W 37a

-15,212-

Weaver, Will

A gravestone made
of wheat

A GRAVESTONE MADE

OF WHEAT

STORIES BY

WILL WEAVER

SIMON AND SCHUSTER

NEW YORK · LONDON · TORONTO · SYDNEY · TOKYO

Simon and Schuster
Simon & Schuster Building
Rockefeller Center
1230 Avenue of the Americas
New York, New York 10020

10 9 8 7 6 5 4 3 2 1

Library of Congress Cataloging-in-Publication Data

Weaver, Will.
    A gravestone made of wheat : stories /
  by Will Weaver.
      p.   cm.
    ISBN 0-671-67097-2
    I. Title.
PS3573.E192G73   1989   88-29699
813'.54—dc 19   CIP

"The Gravestone Made of Wheat" appeared in
Prairie Schooner; "Heart of the Fields" first
appeared in The Hartford Courant; "Going
Home" first appeared in The Minneapolis
Tribune; "Gabriel's Feathers" appeared in
Northern Literary Quarterly; "Dispersal" first ap-
peared in the Chapel Hill Advocate; "From the
Landing" appeared in Selected Stories from
Stanford.

The author wishes to thank the following individuals and institutions for their help: the Bush Foundation for its generous financial support; Bemidji State University; my editor, Allen Peacock, and copy editor, Leslie Ellen; Jonathon Lazear, Stephen Gurney, J. Ruth Stenerson, and, always, Rosalie.

TO MY PARENTS,
HAROLD AND ARLYS WEAVER,
AND THEIR PARENTS.

CONTENTS

A GRAVESTONE MADE
OF WHEAT

"You CAN'T bury your wife here on the farm," the sheriff said. "That's the law."

Olaf Torvik looked up from his chair by the coffin; he did not understand what the sheriff was saying. And why was the sheriff still here, anyway? The funeral was over. They were ready for the burial—a family burial. There should be only Torviks in the living room.

"Do you understand what he's saying, Dad?" Einar said.

Olaf frowned. He looked to his son, to the rest of the family.

"He's saying we can't bury Mom here on the farm," Einar said slowly and deliberately. "He's saying she'll have to be buried in town at Greenacre Cemetery."

Olaf shook his head to clear the gray fuzz of loss, of grief, and Einar's words began to settle into sense. But suddenly a fly buzzed like a chainsaw—near the coffin—inside—there, walking the fine white hair on Inge's right temple. Olaf lurched forward, snatching at the fly in the air but missing. Then he bent over her and licked his thumb and smoothed the hair along her temple. Looking down at Inge, Olaf's mind drew itself together, cleared; he remembered the sheriff.

"Dad?" Einar said.

Olaf nodded. "I'm okay." He turned to the sheriff, John

Carlsen, whom he had known for years and who had been
at the funeral.

"A law?" Olaf said. "What do you mean, John?"

"It's a public health ordinance, Olaf," the sheriff said. "The
state legislature passed it two years ago. It's statewide. I don't
have it with me 'cause I had no idea . . . The law prohibits
home burials."

"The boys and me got her grave already dug," Olaf said.

"I know," the sheriff said. "I saw it at the funeral. That's
why I had to stay behind like this. I mean I hate like hell to
be standing here. You should have told me that's the way you
wanted to bury her, me or the county commissioners or the
judge. Somebody, anyway. Maybe we could have gotten you
a permit or something."

"Nothing to tell," Olaf said, looking across to Einar and
Sarah, to their son Harald and his wife, to Harald's children.
"This is a family affair."

The sheriff took off his wide-brimmed hat and mopped his
forehead with the back of his sleeve. "The times are changing,
Olaf. There's more and more people now, so there's more and
more laws, laws like this one."

Olaf was silent.

"I mean," the sheriff continued, "I suppose I'd like to be
buried in town right in my own backyard under that red maple we got. But what if everybody did that? First thing you
know, people would move away, the graves would go un-
tended and forgotten, and in a few years you wouldn't dare
dig a basement or set a post for fear of turning up somebody's coffin."

"There's eighteen hundred acres to this farm," Olaf said
softly. "That's plenty of room for Inge—and me, too. And nobody in this room is likely to forget where she's buried. None
of us Torviks, anyway."

The sheriff shook his head side to side. "We're talking about
a law here, Olaf. And I'm responsible for the law in this county.
I don't make the laws, you understand, but still I got to en-
force them. That's my job."

Olaf turned and slowly walked across the living room; he stood at the window with his back to the sheriff and the others. He looked out across his farm—the white granaries, the yellow wheat stubble rolling west, and far away, the grove of Norway pine where Inge liked to pick wildflowers in the spring.

"She belongs here on the farm," Olaf said softly.

"I know what you mean," the sheriff said, and began again to say how sorry . . .

Olaf listened but the room came loose, began to drift, compressing itself into one side of his mind, as memories, pictures of Inge pushed in from the past. Olaf remembered one summer evening when the boys were still small and the creek was high and they all went there at sundown after chores and sat on the warm rocks and dangled their white legs in the cold water.

"Dad?" Einar said.

The sheriff was standing close now, as if to get Olaf's attention.

"You been farming here in Hubbard County how long, fifty years?"

Olaf blinked. "Fifty-three years."

"And I've been sheriff over half that time. I know you, I know the boys. None of you has ever broken a law that I can think of, not even the boys. The town folk respect that. . . ."

Olaf's vision cleared and something in him hardened at the mention of town folk. He had never spent much time in town, did not like it there very much. And he believed that, though farmers and townspeople did a lot of business together, it was business of necessity; that in the end they had very little in common. He also had never forgotten how the town folk treated Inge when she first came to Hubbard County.

"What I mean is," the sheriff continued, "you don't want to start breaking the law now when you're seventy-five years old."

"Seventy-eight," Olaf said.

"Seventy-eight," the sheriff repeated.

They were all silent. The sheriff mopped his forehead again. The silence went on for a long time.

Einar spoke. "Say we went ahead with the burial. Here, like we planned."

The sheriff answered to Olaf. "Be just like any other law that was broken. I'd have to arrest you, take you to town. You'd appear before Judge Kruft and plead guilty or not guilty. If you pled guilty, there would be a small fine and you could go home, most likely. Then your wife would be disinterred and brought into town to Greenacre."

"What if he was to plead not guilty?" Einar said.

The sheriff spoke again to Olaf. "The judge would hold a hearing and review the evidence and pass sentence. Or, you could have a trial by jury."

"What do you mean by evidence?" Olaf asked, looking up. That word again after all these years.

The sheriff nodded toward the coffin. "Your wife," he said. "She'd be the evidence."

Evidence . . . evidence; Olaf's mind began to loop back through time, to when Inge first came from Germany and that word meant everything to them. But by force of will Olaf halted his slide into memory, forced his attention to the present. He turned away from the window.

"She told me at the end she should be buried here on the farm," Olaf said softly.

They were all silent. The sheriff removed his hat and ran his fingers through his hair. "Olaf," he said. "I've been here long enough today. You do what you think is best. That's all I'll say today."

THE SHERIFF'S car receded south down the gravel road. His dust hung over the road like a tunnel and Olaf squinted after the car until the sharp July sunlight forced his gaze back into the living room, to his family.

"What are we going to do, Dad?" Einar said.

Olaf was silent. "I . . . need some more time to think," he

said. He managed part of a smile. "Maybe alone here with Inge?"

The others quietly filed through the doorway, but Einar paused, his hand on the doorknob.

"We can't wait too long, Dad," he said quietly.

Olaf nodded. He knew what Einar meant. Inge had died on Wednesday. It was now Friday afternoon, and the scent of the wilting chrysanthemums had been joined by a heavier, sweeter smell.

"I've sent Harald down to Penske's for some ice," Einar said.

Olaf nodded gratefully. He managed part of a smile, and then Einar closed the door to the living room.

OLAF SAT alone by Inge. He tried to order his thoughts, to think through the burial, to make a decision; instead, his mind turned back to the first time he set eyes upon Inge, the day she arrived in Fargo on the Northern Pacific. His mind lingered there and then traveled further back, to his parents in Norway, who had arranged the marriage of Olaf and Inge.

His parents, who had remained and died in Norway, wrote at the end of a letter in June of 1918 about a young German girl who worked for the family on the next farm. They wrote how she wished to come to America; that her family in Germany had been lost in the bombings; that she was dependable and could get up in the morning; that she would make someone a good wife. They did not say what she looked like.

Olaf carried his parents' letter with him for days, stopping now and again in the fields, in the barn, to unfold the damp and wrinkled pages and read the last part again—about the young German girl. He wondered what she looked like. But then again, he was not in a position to be too picky about that sort of thing. It was hard to meet young, unmarried women on the prairie because the farms were so far apart, several miles usually, and at day's end Olaf was too tired to go anywhere, least of all courting. He had heard there were lots of young women in Detroit Lakes and Fargo, but he was not sure how to go about finding one in such large cities. Olaf wrote back to his parents and asked more about the German girl. His parents replied that she would be glad to marry Olaf, if he would have her. He wrote back that he would. His parents never did say what she looked like.

Because of the war, it was nearly two years later, April of 1920, before Olaf hitched up the big gray Belgian to his best wheat wagon, which he had swept as clean as his bedroom floor, and set off to Fargo to meet Inge's train.

It was a long day's ride and there was lots to see—long strings of geese rode the warm winds north, and beyond Detroit Lakes the swells of wheat fields rose up from the snow into black crowns of bare earth. But Olaf kept his eyes to the west, waiting for the first glimpse of Fargo. There were more wagons and cars on the road now, and Olaf stopped nodding to every one as there were far too many. Soon his wagon clattered on paved streets past houses built no more than a fork's handle apart. The Belgian grew skittish and Olaf stopped and put on his blinders before asking the way to the Northern Pacific Railroad station.

Inge's train was to arrive at 3:55 P.M. at the main platform. Olaf checked his watch against the station clock—2:28 P.M.— and then reached under the wagon seat. He brought out the smooth cedar shingle with his name, Olaf Leif Torvik, printed on it in large black letters. He placed it back under the seat, then on second thought, after glancing around the station, slipped the shingle inside his wool shirt. Then he grained and watered the Belgian and sat down to wait.

At 3:58 her train rumbled into the station and slowly drew to a stop, its iron wheels crackling as they cooled. People streamed off the train. Olaf held up his shingle, exchanging a shy grin with another man—John William Olsen—who also held a name-sign.

But there seemed to be few young women on the train, none alone.

A short Dutch-looking woman, small-eyed and thick, came

toward Olaf—but at the last second passed him by. Olaf did not know whether to give thanks or be disappointed. But if the Dutch-looking woman passed him by, so did all the others. Soon Olaf was nearly alone on the platform. No one else descended from the Pullman cars. Sadly, Olaf lowered his shingle. She had not come. He looked at his shingle again, then let it drop to the platform.

He turned back to his wagon. If he was honest with himself, he thought, it all seemed so unlikely anyway; after all, there were lots of men looking for wives, men with more land and money, men certainly better-looking than Olaf.

"Maybe my folks made the mistake of showing her my picture," Olaf said to the Belgian, managing a smile as the horse shook his head and showed his big yellow teeth. Olaf wondered if he would ever take a wife. It seemed unlikely.

Before he unhitched the Belgian, he turned back to the platform for one last look. There, beside the train, staring straight at him, stood a tall, slim girl of about twenty. Her red hair lit the sky. In one hand she clutched a canvas suitcase, and in the other, Olaf's cedar shingle.

INGE ALTENBURG sat straight in Olaf's wagon seat, her eyes scared and straight ahead; she nodded as Olaf explained, in Norwegian, that there was still time today to see about the marriage. She spoke Norwegian with a heavy German accent, said yes, that is what she had come for.

They tried to get married in Fargo, in the courthouse, but a clerk there said that since Olaf was from Minnesota, they should cross the river and try at the courthouse in Moorhead. Olaf explained this to Inge, who nodded. Olaf opened his watch.

"What time do they close in Minnesota?" he asked the clerk.

"Same as here, five o'clock."

It was 4:36; they could still make it today. Olaf kept the Belgian trotting all the way across the Red River Bridge to the Moorhead Courthouse.

Inside, with eight minutes to spare, Olaf found the office of the Justice of the Peace; he explained to the secretary their wish to be married, today, if possible.

The secretary, a white-haired woman with gold-rimmed glasses, frowned.

"It's a bit late today," she said, "but I'll see what I can do. You do have all your papers in order?" she asked of Inge.

"Papers?" Olaf said.

"Her birth certificate and citizenship papers."

Olaf's heart fell. He had not thought of all this. He turned to Inge, who already was reaching under her sweater for the papers. Olaf's hopes soared as quickly as they had fallen.

"All right," the secretary said, examining the birth certificate, "now the citizenship papers."

Inge frowned and looked questioningly at Olaf. Olaf explained the term. Inge held up her hands in despair.

"She just arrived here," Olaf said, "she doesn't have them yet."

"I'm so sorry," the secretary said, and began tidying up her desk.

Olaf and Inge walked out. Inge's eyes began to fill with tears.

"We'll go home to Park Rapids," Olaf told her, "where they know me. There won't be any problem, any waiting, when we get home."

Inge nodded, looking down as she wiped her eyes. Olaf reached out and brushed away a teardrop, the first time he had touched her. She flinched, then burst into real tears.

Olaf drew back his hand, halfway, but then held her at her shoulders with both his hands.

"*Ich verstehe*," he said softly, "I understand."

THEY STAYED that night in a hotel in Detroit Lakes. Olaf paid cash for two single rooms, and they got an early start in the morning. Their first stop was not Olaf's farm, but the Hubbard County Courthouse in Park Rapids.

At the same counter Olaf and Inge applied for both her

citizenship and their marriage license. When Inge listed her
nationality as German, however, the clerk raised an eyebrow
in question. He took her papers back to another, larger office;
the office had a cloudy waved-glass door and Olaf could see
inside, as if underwater, several dark-suited men passing Inge's
papers among themselves and murmuring. After a long time—
thirty-eight minutes—the clerk returned to the counter.

"I'm afraid we have some problems with this citizenship
application," he said to Inge.

When Inge did not reply, the clerk turned to Olaf. "She
speak English?"

"I don't believe so, not much anyway."

"Well, as I said, there are some problems here."

"I can't think of any," Olaf said, "we just want to get married."

"But your wife—er, companion—lists that she's a German
national."

"That's right," Olaf answered, "but she's in America now
and she wants to become an American."

The clerk frowned. "That's the problem—it might not be
so easy. We've got orders to be careful about this sort of
thing."

"What sort of thing?"

"German nationals."

"Germans? Like Inge? But why?"

"You do realize we've been at war with Germany recently?"
the clerk said, pursing his lips. "You read the papers?"

Olaf did not bother to answer.

"I mean the war's over, of course," the clerk said, "but we
haven't received any change orders regarding German nationals."

Olaf laughed. "You think she's a spy or something? This
girl?"

The clerk folded his arms across his chest. Olaf saw that
he should not have laughed, that there was nothing at all to
laugh about.

"We've got our rules," the clerk said.

"What shall we do?" Olaf asked. "What would you recommend?"

The clerk consulted some papers. "For a successful citizenship application she'll need references in the form of letters, letters from people who knew her in Germany and Norway, people who can verify where she was born, where she has worked. We especially need to prove that she was never involved in any capacity in German military or German government work."

"But that might take weeks," Olaf said.

The clerk shrugged. Behind him one of the county commissioners, Sig Hansen, had stopped to listen.

"There's nothing else we can do?" Olaf asked, directing his question beyond the clerk to the commissioner. But Sig Hansen shook his head negatively.

"Sorry, Olaf, that's out of my control. That's one area I can't help you in." The commissioner continued down the hall.

"Sorry," the clerk said, turning to some other papers.

With drawn lips Olaf said, "Thanks for your time."

THEY WAITED for Inge's letters to arrive from Europe. They waited one week, two weeks, five weeks. During this time Olaf slept in the hayloft and Inge took Olaf's bed in the house. She was always up and dressed and had breakfast ready by the time Olaf came in from the barn. Olaf always stopped at the pumphouse, took off his shirt and washed up before breakfast. He usually stepped outside and toweled off his bare chest in the sunlight; once he noticed Inge watching him from the kitchen window.

At breakfast Olaf used his best table manners, making sure to sit straight and hold his spoon correctly. And though they usually ate in silence, the silence was not uncomfortable. He liked to watch her cooking. He liked it when she stood at the wood range with her back to him, flipping pancakes or shaking the skillet of potatoes; he liked the way her body moved, the way strands of hair came loose and curled down her neck. Once she caught him staring. They both looked quickly away, but not before Olaf saw the beginnings of a smile on Inge's face. And it was not long after that, in the evening when it was time for Olaf to retire to the hayloft, that they began to grin foolishly at each other and stay up later and later. Though Olaf was not a religious man, he began to pray for the letters' speedy return.

Then it was July. Olaf was in the field hilling up his corn plants when Inge came running, calling out to him as she came, holding up her skirts for speed, waving a package in her free hand. It was from Norway. They knelt in the hot dirt and tore open the wrapping. The letters! Three of them. They had hoped for more, just to make sure, but certainly three would be enough.

Olaf and Inge did not even take time to hitch up the wagon, but rode together bareback on the Belgian to Park Rapids. They ran laughing up the courthouse steps, Olaf catching Inge's hand on the way. Once inside, however, they made themselves serious and formal, and carefully presented the letters to the clerk. The clerk examined them without comment.

"I'll have to have the Judge look at these," he said, "he's the last word on something like this." The clerk then retreated with their letters down the hall and out of sight.

The Judge took a long time with the letters. Twenty minutes. Thirty-nine minutes. Olaf and Inge waited at the clerk's window, holding hands below the cool granite counter. As they waited, Inge began to squeeze Olaf's hand with increasing strength until her fingers dug into his palm and hurt him; he did not tell her, however. Finally the clerk returned. He handed back the letters.

"I'm sorry," he said, "but the Judge feels these letters are not sufficient."

Olaf caught the clerk's wrist. The clerk's eyes jumped wide and round and scared; he tried to pull back his arm but Olaf had him.

"We want to get married, that's all," he said hoarsely.

"Wait—" the clerk stammered, his voice higher now, "maybe you should see the Judge yourselves."

"That's a damned good idea," Olaf said. He let go of the clerk's arm. The clerk rubbed his wrist and pointed down the hall.

Olaf and Inge entered the Judge's chambers, and Olaf's hopes plummeted. All the old books, the seals under glass on the walls, the papers; the white hair and expressionless face of the Judge himself: they all added up to power, to right-of-way. The Judge would have it his way.

Olaf explained their predicament. The Judge nodded impatiently and flipped through the letters again.

"Perhaps what we should do for you," the Judge said, "is to have you wait on this application for a period of say, one calendar year. If, during that time, it is determined that Inge Altenburg is loyal and patriotic, then we can consider her for citizenship. And, of course, marriage."

"One year!" Olaf exclaimed.

The Judge drew back and raised his eyebrows. Sig Hansen, the commissioner, had paused in the doorway. He shook his head at the Judge.

"Christ, Herb," he said, "you ought to run it through, let 'em get married. They're harmless. They're just farmers."

Inge rose up from her chair. There was iron in her face. "Come—" she commanded Olaf, in English, "it is time we go to home."

THEY RODE HOME slowly, silently. The Belgian sensed their sorrow and kept turning his wide brown eyes back to Olaf. But Olaf had no words for the big animal. Inge held Olaf around his waist. As they came in sight of their buildings she leaned her head on his shoulder and he could feel her crying.

They ate their dinner in silence, and then Olaf returned to his cornfield. At supper they were silent again.

COME SUNDOWN, Olaf climbed the ladder to the hayloft and unrolled his bedroll in the hay. He wished he could have found some good thing to say at supper, but it was not in him. Not tonight. Olaf felt old, tired beyond his thirty-three years. He lay back on the loose prairie hay and watched the sun set in the knotholes of the west barn wall, red, then violet, then purple, then blue shrinking to gray. He hardly remembered going to sleep. But then he knew he must be dreaming. For standing above him, framed in the faint moonlight of the loft, stood Inge. She lay down beside him in the hay and when her hair fell across his face and neck he knew he could not be dreaming. He also knew that few dreams could ever be better than this. And in his long life with Inge, none were.

Olaf rose from his chair by her casket. That night when she came to him in the loft was forty-five years past. That night was Olaf's last in the hayloft, for they considered themselves married, come morning—married by body, by heart, and by common law.

And Inge never forgot her treatment at the Hubbard County Courthouse in Park Rapids; she rarely shopped in the town, preferring instead Detroit Lakes, which was twelve miles farther but contained no unpleasant memories.

Nor did she become a citizen; she remained instead without file or number, nonexistent to federal, state, or local records. She was real, Olaf thought, only to those who knew her, who loved her. And that, Olaf suddenly understood, was the way she should remain. As in her life, her death.

Before Olaf called the family back into the room, he thought he should try to pray. He got down on his knees on the wood floor by the coffin and folded his hands. He waited, but no words came. He wondered if he had forgotten how to pray. Olaf knew that he believed in a great God of some kind. He had trouble with Jesus, but with God there was no question. He ran into God many times during the year: felt of him in the warm field-dirt of May; saw his face in the shiny harvest grain; heard his voice among the tops of the Norway pines. But he was not used to searching him out, to calling for him.

Nor could he now. Olaf found he could only cry. Long, heaving sobs and salty tears that dripped down his wrists to the floor. He realized, with surprise, that this was the first time he had cried since Inge's death; that his tears in their free flowing were a kind of prayer. He realized, too, that God was with him these moments. Right here in this living room.

WHEN THE FAMILY reassembled, Olaf told them his decision. He spoke clearly, resolutely.

"We will bury Inge here on the farm as we planned," he said, "but in a little different fashion."

He outlined what they would do, asked if anyone disagreed, if there were any worries. There were none. "All right then, that's settled," Olaf said. He looked around the room at his family—Einar, Sarah, the children, the others.

"And do you know what else we should do?" Olaf said.

No one said anything.

"Eat!" Olaf said. "I'm mighty hungry."

The others laughed, and the women turned to the kitchen. Soon they all sat down to roast beef, boiled potatoes with butter, dill pickles, wheat bread, strong black coffee, and pie. During lunch Harald returned with the ice. Einar excused himself from the table and went to help Harald.

Once he returned and took from a cupboard some large black plastic garbage bags. Olaf could hear them working in the living room, and once Einar said, "Don't let it get down along her side, there."

Olaf did not go into the living room while they worked. He poured himself another cup of coffee, which, strangely, made him very tired. He tried to remember when he had slept last.

Sarah said to him, "Perhaps you should rest a little bit before we . . ."

Olaf nodded. "You're right," he said, "I'll go upstairs and lie down a few minutes. Just a few minutes."

OLAF STARTED awake at the pumping thuds of the John Deere starting. He sat up quickly—too quickly, nearly pitching over, and pushed aside the curtain. It was late—nearly dark. How could he have slept so long? It was time.

He hurriedly laced his boots and pulled on a heavy wool jacket over his black suit-coat. Downstairs, the women and children were sitting in the kitchen, dressed and waiting for him.

"We would have wakened you," Sarah said.

Olaf grinned. "I thought for a minute there . . ." Then he buttoned his coat and put on a woolen cap. He paused at the door. "One of the boys will come for you when everything is ready," he said to Sarah.

"We know," she said.

Outside, the sky was bluish purple and Harald was running the little John Deere tractor in the cow lot. The tractor carried a front-end loader and Harald was filling the scoop with fresh manure. Beyond the tractor some of the Black Angus stretched stiffly and snorted at the disturbance. Harald drove out of the lot when the scoop was rounded up and dripping. He stopped by the machine shed, went inside, and returned with two bags of commercial nitrogen fertilizer.

"Just to make sure, Grandpa," he said. His smile glinted white in the growing dark.

"Won't hurt," Olaf said. Then he tried to think of other things they would need.

"Rope," Olaf said. "And a shovel." Then he saw both on the tractor.

"Everything's ready," Harald said, pointing to the little John Deere. "She's all yours. We'll follow."

Olaf climbed up to the tractor's seat and then backed away from the big machine-shed doors. Einar and Harald rolled open the mouth of the shed and went inside.

The noise of their two big tractors still startled Olaf, even in daylight, and he backed up farther as the huge, dual-tandem John Deeres rumbled out of their barn. A single tire on them, he realized, was far bigger than the old Belgian he used to have. And maybe that's why he never drove the big tractors. Actually, he'd never learned, hadn't wished to. He left them to the boys, who drove them as easily as Olaf drove the little tractor. Though they always frightened him a little, Olaf's long wheat fields called for them—especially tonight. Behind each of the big tractors, like an iron spine with twelve shining ribs, rode a plow.

Olaf led the caravan of tractors. They drove without lights into the eighty-acre field directly west from the yellow-lit living-room window of the house. At what he sensed was the middle of the field, Olaf halted. He lowered the manure and fertilizer onto the ground. Then, with the front-end digger, he began to unearth Inge's grave.

Einar and Harald finished the sides of the grave with shovels. Standing out of sight in the hole, their showers of dirt pumped rhythmically up and over the side. Finished, they climbed up and brushed themselves off, and then walked back to the house for the others.

Olaf waited alone by the black hole. He stared down into its darkness and realized that he probably would not live long after Inge, and yet felt no worry or fear. For he realized there was, after all, a certain order to the events and times of his life: all the things he had worked for and loved were now nearly present.

Behind, he heard the faint rattle of the pickup. He turned to watch it come across the field toward the grave. Its bumper glinted in the moonlight, and behind, slowly walking, came the dark shapes of his family. In the bed of the pickup was Inge's coffin.

The truck stopped alongside the grave. Einar turned off the engine and then he and Harald lifted the coffin out and onto the ground. The family gathered around. Sarah softly sang "Rock of Ages," and then they said together the Twenty-third Psalm. Olaf could not speak past "The Lord is my . . ."

Then it was over. Einar climbed onto the tractor and raised the loader over the coffin. Harald tied ropes to the loader's arms and looped them underneath and around the coffin. Einar raised the loader until the ropes tightened and lifted the long dark box off the ground. Harald steadied the coffin, kept it from swinging, as Einar drove forward until the coffin was over the dark hole. Olaf stepped forward toward it as if to—to what?

Einar turned questioningly toward Olaf. "Now, Dad?" he said.

Olaf nodded.

Swaying slightly in the moonlight, the coffin slowly sank into the grave. There was a scraping sound as it touched bottom. Harald untied the ropes and then Einar began to push forward the mound of earth; the sound of dirt thumping on the coffin seemed to fill the field. When the grave was half filled, Einar backed the tractor to the pile of manure and pushed it forward into the hole. Harald carried the two bags of nitrogen fertilizer to the grave, slit their tops, and poured them in after the manure. Then Einar filled in the earth and scattered what was left over until the grave was level with the surrounding field.

Olaf tried to turn away, but could not walk. For with each step he felt the earth rising up to meet his boots as if he were moving into some strange room, an enormous room, one that went on endlessly. He thought of his horses, his old team. He heard himself murmur some word that only they would understand.

"Come Dad," Sarah said, taking Olaf by the arm. "It's over."

Olaf let himself be led into the pickup. Sarah drove him and the children to the field's edge by the house where Einar had parked the little John Deere.

"You coming inside now?" Sarah asked as she started the children toward the house.

"No, I'll wait here until the boys are finished," Olaf said, "you go on ahead."

Even as he spoke the big tractors rumbled alive. Their running lights flared on and swung around as Einar and Harald drove to the field's end near Olaf. They paused there a moment, side by side, as their plows settled onto the ground. Then their engine RPMs came up and the tractors, as one, leaned into their work and headed straight downfield toward Inge's grave.

The furrows rolled up shining in the night light. Olaf knew this earth. It was heavy soil, had never failed him. He knew also that next year, and nearly forever after, there would be one spot in the middle of the field where the wheat grew greener, taller, and more golden than all the rest. It would be the gravestone made of wheat.

Olaf sat on the little tractor in the darkness until the boys had plowed the field black from side to side. Then they put away the tractors and fed the Angus. After that they ate breakfast, and went to bed at dawn.

DISPERSAL

To GET TO the Matson sale I had to drive through town. On the edge of town I passed the red brick high school where my wife, Ellen, teaches English in the upper grades. Through the school windows I could see students moving about in front of colored posters. I knew that if Ellen weren't teaching I could not be thinking about buying that New Holland hay mower listed on Matson's sale bill. My forty Holsteins are a fine bunch of cows, but if it weren't for Ellen's town job, things on the farm would be tough.

Which made me think of Matson and his family. I didn't really know them—they were strangers to me—but I could tell from their sale bill what had gone wrong. Too much machinery, not enough wheat. Too many bankers, not enough rain. Tough luck all around.

But bad luck draws a crowd like blood pulls flies. Several pickups followed mine as I turned at the red auction flags. Soon up ahead I could see the shiny aluminum tops of Matson's grain bins. Below stood his newer white house and, beside it, lines of pickups stretched from his yard down his driveway and along the shoulders of the highway.

I parked, leaving myself room to turn around, and began to

walk quickly toward the crowd. Sales do that to you. Anything can happen at a sale. In Matson's yard cars and trucks had parked on his lawn. Their tires rutted the soggy April grass and water welled up in the zigzag tread marks. Closer to his house, a pickup had backed over a small trimmed spruce tree. The tree remained bent over in a green horseshoe beneath the tire. I slowed my walk. For a moment I thought of turning back, of going home. If everybody left, there could be no sale. But even as I thought, several farmers passed me. I kept walking.

Ahead, the crowd surrounded the auctioneer, who stood atop a hayrack. He wore a wide black cowboy hat, and his tanned, wrinkled throat bobbed like a rooster's craw as he cried the small stuff. Cans of nails. Some rusty barbed wire. Three fence posts. Some half-cans of herbicide. A broken shovel. Beyond the auctioneer, in even lines, was the machinery, mostly John Deere green and Massey-Ferguson red. Beyond everything were Matson's long, unplowed fields.

I registered for a bidder's number, then stood in the sunlight with a cup of coffee and looked over the crowd. You shouldn't get in a hurry at a sale. You ought to get the feel of things. The crowd was mostly farmers with a few bankers and real estate men thrown in. The younger bankers wore flannel shirts and seed-corn caps, but I could pick them out right away. Like the real estate guys, their faces were white and smooth and they squinted a lot, as if they were moles who just today had crawled out of the ground into the sunlight. Moles or skunks.

Off to the side I noticed an older farmer picking through a box of odds and ends. He fished out a rat-tail file from the box and drew it across his thumbnail. He glanced briefly around, then laid the file alongside the box and continued digging.

"Gonna spend some of the wife's money?" somebody said to me. I turned. It was Jim Hartley, who milked cows just down the road from my farm. I knew he already had a good mower.

"Not if she can help it," I said.

He grinned. But then his forehead wrinkled and his blue eyes turned serious. "Hell of a deal, a bank sale like this. Imag-

ine if you had to sell out. Had all these people come onto your
farm and start picking through your stuff like crows on road
kill."

I looked back at the old man with the file. But both he and
it were gone.

"Be tough," I said. That old bastard.

Hartley looked around at the crowd. "Haven't seen Matson
anywhere. And I can't blame him for that. Good day to get
drunk."

"I don't really know the man," I said. "He's a stranger to me."

"He's got some pretty fair equipment," Hartley said. "The
combine looks good. And that New Holland mower—it's damn
near brand new." He narrowed his eyes. "You could use a
good mower."

"Maybe I'll take a look," I said. I raised my coffee cup, took
a sip.

Soon enough Hartley went off toward the combine, and I
found the mower. From a distance it looked good. The yellow
and red colors were still bright, which meant it had always
been shedded. Up close I checked the cutting sickle. All the
knives were in place and still showed serration, which was like
buying good used tires still showing the little rubber teats on
the face of their tread. Next I turned the hay pickup reel to
watch the sickle move. The knives slid easily between their
guards with a sound that reminded me of Ellen's good pinking
shears. Then I saw the toolbox and the mower's maintenance
manual. The thin book was tattered and spotted with grease
and with Matson's fingerprints, tiny whirlwinds painted in oil.
Its pages fell open to the lubrication section. There Matson
had circled and numbered every one of the grease fittings. I
was sold.

I stashed the manual and walked away. I didn't want to lin-
ger near the mower and attract other bidders. I bought another
cup of coffee and then stood off to the side where I could
watch the mower and see who stopped by it. Two men paused
by the mower, but they wore wheat seed-caps and smoked,
which said they were grain men. Soon they moved on to the

combine. One stocky farmer slowed by the mower, but he wore high rubber boots and a Purina "Pig-Power" jacket. I was feeling lucky until a man and his son walked toward the mower like it was a magnet and they were nails. Their cuffs were spotted with manure splash. They wore loose bib overalls for easy bending. And they wore caps cocked to one side, a habit dairymen have from leaning their foreheads against the flanks of their cows.

The son turned the pickup reel while the old man held his ear to the main bearing case. After the old man nodded, the two of them crawled underneath the mower and didn't come out for a long time. What the hell did they see under there? Finally they came out and stood off to the side. They stared at the mower and nodded and whispered. I wondered how many cows they milked.

By now the auctioneer was in the back of his pickup and was barking his way along the hay wagons and rakes, headed this way. I went over my figures again. I knew in town that mower would sell for $5,500, give or take a couple of hundred. I had set my limit at $5,000. As long as I stuck to that figure I couldn't go wrong.

"Now here's a mighty clean mower—" the auctioneer called. The hook and pull of his arms drew the crowd forward. "Boys, if this mower were a car, we'd call her 'cherry.' You know what this mower would sell for in town, boys, so somebody give me six thousand to start!"

The crowd was silent.

"Five thousand, then!"

Still there was silence.

"Boys, boys—four thousand to start!"

In the silence somewhere a dog barked. The auctioneer's eyes flickered to the clerk and then to the banker. The banker, ever so slightly, shrugged. He was worried about the big tractors and combines, about the house and the land.

"Boys, this ain't a rummage sale, but somebody give a thousand dollars."

I saw the younger dairyman nod, and the bidding was on. At

$1,600, it was between the dairyman and me. The young fellow began to look at his father before each bid. At $1,750 I saw the old man fold his arms and squint. At $1,850 he pursed his lips and shook his head. His son mouthed a silent curse and looked down.

"Eighteen hundred three times—gone!" the auctioneer said and pointed to me. I held up my bidder's number for the clerk to record as the crowd dissolved away to the next implement.

I couldn't believe my luck. Eighteen hundred was a steal, no two ways about that. My ears burned. I felt shaky. I sat down on the mower's long drawbar. I ran my hand along its cold steel. I wondered for a moment if the mower had felt any change, if it knew I was up there. Soon enough that shaky feeling gave way to a stronger idea—that I had to get that mower out of here and home as soon as possible.

I found the clerk's booth and wrote out my check. Then I brought around my truck and got ready to hook on to the mower. Trouble was, Matson had parked the mower in field-cutting position, which meant its mouth was too wide for highway travel. I knew that the drawbar released to swing to a narrower stance. But for the life of me I could not see how. I knew I still wasn't completely over that shaky feeling because if I had been home on my own farm and just sat there a few minutes, I could have figured things out. Not here, though.

I asked another farmer if he knew, but the man was in a hurry to join the crowd around the combine. So there was only one thing to do—find someone who knew for sure. And that was Matson.

I walked up to his house. The drapes were all drawn. I rapped on the door and waited. Inside, I could hear a baby crying. Along the sidewalk was a flower bed. Somebody last fall had done a lot of work planting tulip bulbs, but now their first green spears were drowned in quack grass.

A woman answered the door. She was about Ellen's age, late thirties. She had a bone-white face that said she seldom went outside.

"Is Mr. Matson home?" I asked.

"Yes," she said. She just stood there, looking beyond me to the auction. From deeper in the house I could smell cigarette smoke.

"I bought . . . an implement," I said.

Her pale eyes returned to mine. "Tom—" she called back to the dusk of the hallway.

We waited. There was no answer. No one came forward. She shrugged. "He's back there in the living room," she said, leaning toward the now louder crying of the baby. "Why don't you go on in?"

I walked down the dim hallway into the living room. In the room the TV was a colored bull's-eye. The Phil Donahue show was on, but the picture kept wavering, then skipping ahead several frames. I didn't see Matson anywhere.

"Tom," his wife said loudly from behind me. "Some man's got a question."

Matson slowly sat up. He'd been lying on the couch, on his back. He was fully dressed in coveralls, leather boots, a cap, even his work gloves. He did not take his eyes off the TV.

"And why should we believe you?" Donahue was saying to a man seated on the stage.

"Tom—" his wife said even louder this time.

"I heard," he said.

"The mower," I began. "I bought the mower and . . ."

Matson nodded and walked past me toward the door. I followed. Outside we walked in silence toward the mower. The auctioneer was standing on the platform of the combine. "Boys, I'll buy this combine myself," he was saying. "Then I'll put it on a truck and I'll haul it to North Dakota and I'll make myself ten thousand dollars in one day. Any one of you could do the same thing, you know that, boys."

Matson did not look at the auctioneer. He walked toward the mower like there was a perfectly straight but invisible line drawn in the dirt. I explained my trouble with the drawbar. He nodded and slid underneath. I saw him remove three cotter keys. He handed them to me, then swung the drawbar.

"Now why didn't I see that?" I said.

But Matson still didn't speak. He just stared at the mower.

"It looks like a good mower," I said, then wished I hadn't. I was sure he would ask me how much I had paid.

He was silent. Then, without looking up from the mower, he said, "I'll hook you on."

"You bet," I answered. I got in my pickup. He waved me backwards, then held up his hands. I felt him slide the iron pin through the mower's tongue and my bumper hitch, felt the clank in my spine. You know when you're hooked on.

I got out of the pickup again but there was not much to say.

"I appreciate the help," I said.

But Matson didn't reply. He just stared at the iron pin that joined his mower to my truck.

I drove off very slowly, watching the mower and Matson in the rearview mirror. It was like they were on TV. The mower stayed the same size, but Matson got smaller and smaller as the camera pulled away from him.

Suddenly Matson's legs began to move. They moved faster and faster, and Matson grew in size in my mirror. Then he was running alongside my truck, pounding on the side with his fist. Ahead of me was the highway, and I thought of speeding up and leaving him behind. But I stopped. I rolled my window halfway down.

Matson's face was completely white. He paused as if he had forgotten why he had run after me. Then he said, "It was a good mower." His right eye twitched as he spoke.

"I believe that," I said.

"It never let me down," he said.

"That's because you took good care of it," I said. "That's plain to see."

"I did," Matson said. "I worked hard. Nobody can take that away from me," he said. His voice was softer now. I could hardly hear him.

"Nobody I know ever said otherwise," I answered. "When your name came up people said, 'Matson—with a little more luck, some more rain, better wheat prices, he'd have made it.' That's what I heard other people say."

"This is not my fault," he said, swinging his arm at the pick-ups, at the whole auction. "—It wasn't me."

For one long moment I thought of getting out of my pickup and putting my arms around Matson. But you just can't do things like that. We waited there. Finally he turned away.

OUT ON THE highway, I kept the truck at twenty-five. The mower started to sway side to side if I drove any faster. Ahead of me the sun was shining on the dark fields where other farmers were planting. I couldn't stop thinking about Matson. About that run-over spruce tree. His white-faced wife, her tulip bed run to weeds.

I thought about Ellen, about how sometimes in the evenings when there's nothing on TV she reads me poems, poems she likes and uses in her English classes. I thought of one poem in particular, by W. H. Auden. His poem was about a painting in a museum, a painting of Icarus and Daedalus. Even I remembered that story from school. Icarus and Daedalus were prisoners on this island, and they made wings from feathers and wax, strapped on the wings, and flew away. Icarus, however, flew too close to the sun, and the heat melted the wax from his feathers and he fell into the ocean and drowned. In the painting there was a plowman in a nearby field. The plowman saw Icarus fall but he just kept plowing. There was a passing ship, too, but it had somewhere to get to and so it just kept sailing.

Suddenly my truck yawed and shuddered. Behind me the mower was whipping violently side to side—I was driving way over fifty. I hit the brakes hard. Back at twenty-five, the mower trailed straight again. I let out a breath and watched my speedometer from then on.

But I hated driving that slowly. What I most wanted to do was get the mower home, park it in the machine shed, and close the door on it. Then I wanted to eat lunch, sweep up in the barn, feed silage, milk, eat supper, watch the weather report, and go to bed. Because once I had done all those things, this day would be over.

GABRIEL'S FEATHERS

"SAY GOOD-BYE to your father," Timmy's mother said.

Timmy watched her latch the big suitcase, then run twine through the handles. His father was in the barn, waiting, but Timmy remained by the suitcase. He picked at one of the corners and watched his fingernail fill up with tiny slivers of cardboard. His mother knotted the twine, then turned to him again.

"Please," she said. She reached and touched his face. He smelled soap on her fingers, the clean vinegary scent of her brown hair. "Go tell him good-bye," she said. "It will help Mommy."

In the silence a cricket chirped from somewhere under the cupboards.

"I'll get him—" Timmy cried. He ran and grabbed up the kitchen broom, but his mother caught its handle as he passed. For a moment they pulled against each other; he could feel her through the wood.

"Timmy," she said, "the quicker you say good-bye, the sooner we can get away."

Timmy was silent.

"You want to go, I know you do," she said.

Timmy stared at a space beside his mother. It was a habit of his, looking not at people but at the empty space where they had just been.

39

"Jacobsen and the other boys," his mother said, "you have fun with them. You always like it once we get there."

Timmy nodded his head in a circular motion that meant both yes and no. It was an answer, he had found, that kept away more questions. It was an answer that let people fill in their own ideas, an answer that kept him from having to take sides with his mother or with his father. But he was ten. He was ten years old and he knew that someday soon he would have to choose between them.

LUGGING the suitcase, Timmy stepped outside. The high blue sky was striped white with jet trails. He squinted up at them. There were always jet trails over South Dakota because there were underground missiles around somewhere. The planes and the missiles were connected. At school he often heard the word *radar*, but he did not know what it meant, and did not ask because asking was risky. Asking called attention. Attention was danger. Anyway, he knew on his own that radar was like radio, a radio with the sound turned off. Radar was all around everybody all the time. Radar couldn't be heard or seen, but it was there.

Timmy crossed the yard with his face turned up to the sky. There were more jet trails today than he'd ever seen. With a hand over one eye and then switching to the other eye he followed the lengthening trails, trying to spot the lighter blue speck of the jet plane that kept unwinding and unwinding the thin strings of smoke. Two of the white strings angled toward each other, and he stopped walking. The stripes touched; he caught his breath. Then the white lines continued in a widening X, and he let out the air.

Timmy looked back toward the house. His mother stood at the screen door, her hand shading her eyes, watching him. He leaned the suitcase against the truck and walked slowly on to the barn.

While his eyes adjusted to the dim light of chicken barn, Timmy kept his hand on the door. White chickens fluttered into focus, then the high, dark layers of caging. Then his father.

His father, a thin man in dark coveralls, sat bent forward over the wing-clipper machine with a box of yellow chicks. He straightened to look at Timmy, then reached to shut off the motor. He pulled off his leather gloves one finger at a time and at the same time ran his eyes down Timmy's clean clothes. His ironed pants. "All dressed up," his father said. "You must be going somewhere."

Timmy's heart skipped once like the tiny wind-devils that twisted and whirled through the yard. "Yessir," he said.

"And where would that be?"

Timmy swallowed. "Church camp," he whispered.

His father stared for a long time. Then he said, "I suppose she's got the house all cleaned up?"

Timmy nodded his yes-and-no nod.

"Yessir, you can always tell when church camp rolls around," his father said. Without looking down he spit into the straw.

Timmy stared at the space beside his father.

"She leave any food?" his father said.

Timmy blinked. His own voice sounded small and faraway. "Yes."

"What food?"

"Two pies. Bread."

"But she's taking more than that," his father said.

Timmy was silent for a nothing moment. "A sack of potatoes, some squash."

"More than that," his father said.

"Some canned stuff. Jelly."

His father took off his cap and ran his hand through his hair. His face was brown, his forehead white. "You see, Timboy, she takes more to her church folks than she leaves for us," his father said.

Timmy said nothing.

His father squinted. "What if there weren't enough spuds and squash left for us this winter? Then what?"

Timmy stared. He stood straight, tipped slightly back, staring without blinking; he thought of the old red Massey-Ferguson tractor behind the machine shed, of how swallows sometimes flew through the empty space where its engine had been.

"So go to camp, then," his father said, narrowing his eyes. "But watch yourself. It's easy for them preachers to get their hooks into you when they've got you right there for three days straight. You understand what I mean."

Timmy nodded quickly.

His father stared at him for a moment. "You're ten now," his father said.

"Almost eleven," Timmy said.

His father nodded. "What I'm saying, son, is when you're down there at that church camp, you remember what I always told you."

Son. Sun. Son. Timmy felt the empty part, the space through which he let things pass, begin to fill. It filled with something he could not name, something he both wanted and did not want.

"So what do I always tell you?" his father asked.

"Believe-nothing-what-you-hear-and-only-half-what-you-see," Timmy answered in a rush.

His father nodded. A half-smile grew in his thin lips. But then his eyes clouded. He stared toward the door and was silent for a long time.

"You see, Tim-boy, your mother, she was a different woman when we were first married. Before she got religion. We thought the same. We did things together. We'd go out on the town once in a while, like down to the Missile Toe Inn on a Saturday night. I'd take a drink or two. Your mother, she'd never let me buy her a drink, but she'd sip out of my glass. Her cheeks would get redder than Prairie Spy apples, and we'd dance some and laugh. On the way home we'd drive across the prairie with the windows down, the wind blowing chilly and the stars bright."

His father's voice drew to silence. He looked up suddenly, as if he had forgotten Timmy was standing there.

"That's all gone now, Tim-boy. She's gone."

Timmy was silent.

"Those damn preachers got her. And you're all that's left."

Timmy waited.

His father narrowed his eyes again. Timmy tried to empty himself, but he was not quick enough.

"She got you prayin' again?" his father said.

"No—" Timmy said. He swallowed and looked down at the straw.

"You think prayin' does any good?" his father said.

"I . . . don't know," Timmy answered.

The barn door squeaked and sunlight flared behind the black shape of Timmy's mother. She stepped inside. "You run along to the pickup," she said to Timmy. "Get inside."

IN THE SUNLIGHT, his ear to the hot wood of the barn door, Timmy listened.

". . . last year of church camp for him," his father said. Timmy heard him spit. "He's plenty big enough to lend a hand around the farm now. He can't learn anything about this farm when he's in church all the time."

"Not all the time," Timmy's mother said. Her voice was quiet; Timmy could hardly hear her. "Just Sunday mornings and then camp once a year."

"Church camp ain't good for a young kid like him. It puts too much religion on him too fast," his father said.

His mother was silent.

"He'll get funny ideas about life," Timmy's father said, "like all you got to do is pray for something and the next day it comes in the mail."

"Praying never hurt anybody," his mother said.

"Neither did spitting into the wind."

"Praying never hurt, anybody can do it."

"Anybody—" his father said, his voice faster, harder, like an engine beginning to race, "you mean *me*, don't you? Well, you want to know why I don't pray?"

"I know, I know," Timmy's mother said. Her voice was one tone, like a record repeating.

"—Because the world is dog-eat-dog, that's why. You live by your own two hands. If you want something, then you got to do it by yourself or make it by yourself 'cause no one else is going to do it for you. They're looking out for their own selves. And praying? Praying is like—like wishing, only worse. You sit around hoping and praying and turning the other cheek for another slap like you always say, and pretty soon not only have you got nothing to show for it, you got no head to turn because they've slapped it clean off."

Timmy's mother said something that Timmy couldn't hear. Something low and toneless to herself.

"Praying," Timmy's father said, and spit again. "Everything works better without it."

ON THE HIGHWAY, Timmy's mother drove hunched over the steering wheel as if she were pulling herself forward down the road. From the side of his eyes, Timmy watched her foot flex on the gas pedal. He saw the rubber skirt around the stickshift swell, sink, then swell again from the truck's fast, unsteady speed.

When the fence posts of his father's farm gave way to those of the neighbor's, Timmy's mother gradually leaned back from the wheel. The truck slowed. They drove on in silence. After a while his mother blew her nose and wiped her eyes with a handkerchief. She looked over at Timmy.

"He's a Godless man, Timmy. He's a hard-hearted man . . ." She wiped her eyes again. They were silent. Timmy counted twelve telephone poles.

"What did he say to you?" she asked. Her eyes were red.

Timmy was silent a moment. "To watch myself," he said.

His mother shook her head sadly. "Your father doesn't know Jesus. He doesn't know Jesus and he no longer knows us."

She looked over at him, tears welling again. "The devil has got ahold of your father, Timmy. He's lost to us. But I've got Jesus." She wiped her eyes and smiled at him. "Jesus and you."

Timmy said nothing. He turned away from his mother and looked out his window at the passing prairie. He began to watch for the little sparrow hawks that sat on the telephone wires. Always at the last moment before the truck drew even, the little hawks fell away from the wire. Fell away free. The white undersides of their wings broke their fall, and in a moment they were speeding low across the prairie.

AFTER THEY passed the town of Groton, Timmy began to watch for the Missile Toe Inn. The Missile Toe was an old Pullman diner car that had been hauled in and made into a restaurant when the soldiers were working on the missile silos. It sat alongside the highway on a short section of railroad that went no farther than either end of the diner. Now, up ahead, Timmy could see the Missile Toe.

"Remember?" Timmy's mother said.

Timmy nodded. He remembered the soldiers and construction workers sitting at the counter, eating, laughing, using words that brought a grin from his father and a giggle from his mother. He heard again the spitting sound of hamburgers on the grill, and the metallic snarl of the malted mixer rod when it spun against the cylinder, the clink of glasses and of silverware on heavy plates. He smelled oil and gasoline and chemicals on the coveralls of the construction workers, and the thicker smell of onion rings and deep fat fryers. He remembered the fainter, violet scent of his mother's perfume; he wondered where the little bottle had gone. Had she poured it down the sink? Did its blue water, swirling on the white porcelain, leave a stain? Most of all he remembered the laughing, easy voices of his mother and father.

But now the Missile Toe leaned to the west, where its ties had sunk in the sand. The glass was broken in every windowpane. Classes from different high schools had painted their graduation years across the diner and across each other in a rainbow of colors; their paint was faded by the sun and, like the entire diner, peppered rusty by the blasts of passing shotguns.

The pickup passed several more telephone poles. Timmy stared across the fields. "Where are the missiles?" Timmy asked.

"I don't know," his mother answered. "Not many people do. Somewhere close, though."

Timmy looked out across the soilbank land. It was brown and flat far away.

"What's radar?"

Timmy's mother thought a moment. "It's . . . electricity, like waves of electricity in the sky. Radar watches out for us, listens, protects us from our enemies." She turned to him and smiled. "Like God."

Timmy turned to look at his mother, then turned back to his window. "But you can't see it. Like you can't see God," he said.

"God sees us, though—" his mother said quickly. She reached across and smoothed his forehead with her hand. "He sees us every minute of our lives."

Timmy said nothing. He looked at his mother briefly, then turned back to his window. He thought about God.

About his mother and father.

About the missiles and the radar.

About everything. But all of it at once made his mind spin, and he had to close his eyes to stop thinking. He kept them closed. He leaned back against his seat and let the tire sounds run through him.

When Timmy awoke, the sun had moved to the side window of the truck. He had sweated where his back touched the seat, and his skin was cold. He did not remember his dream.

The flat, open prairie was gone. Now the truck droned past fields of wheat that swelled up and down in long slopes of yellow. Sometimes the wheat land gave way to rolling cornfields dotted with small sloughs where mallards dipped for food. Cattails grew in the ditches, and drooped top-heavy with red-winged blackbirds. As the pickup passed, the blackbirds flared up. Cattail fuzz sprayed from their feet, then hung shining in the sunlight. After the pickup was past, the blackbirds slanted back to their perches, sharp feet reaching.

"Not much farther now," his mother said. She was leaning toward the window glass again.

They turned off the highway onto gravel. Small stones clattered in the wheel wells. Ahead was another car, and soon two more were behind. Dust hung and he could not see far ahead or behind, only to the next car. The cars were full of people and carried suitcases tied on top. Timmy's stomach began to tighten.

Ahead was a grove of red oaks. As they passed the trees, his mother leaned forward until her forehead touched glass. She sucked in her breath. Late afternoon sunlight glinted on long, even lines of cars spread over several acres of a hayfield. Beyond the cars the green top of the cook tent rose up like a circus tent; in fact, strangers sometimes thought it all was a circus, and drove in. They usually left quickly, however, at the sight of so many people all carrying black Bibles.

To the left of the cook tent was the long white woman's dormitory where Timmy always slept on a straw tick alongside his mother's bed. His stomach tightened even more as he thought of the long, open hall of ticks; the old women undressing for bed; their praying, their muttering. He hoped he and his mother could find ticks near the door this year.

They parked. His mother switched off the key and the truck's engine died. Timmy made no move to get out.

"Come on now," his mother said, "I'll bet you run into your friend, that Jacobsen boy, right away."

Jacobsen. Timmy had forgotten about Jacobsen. But still he opened the truck door slowly.

One of the parking-lot boys came up. He leaned to look into the rear, then started to unload the potatoes and squash. "Figured you'd need a hand," he said to Timmy's mother. "Just the two of you."

"Thank you," Timmy's mother said.

The boy was tall and thin, and his face was scrubbed so

clean there were red chapped spots on his cheekbones. As another car passed he murmured, "They just keep coming."

"The Lord's family gets bigger every year," Timmy's mother said. She looked out across the field of cars. The sun gleamed in her eyes. She let out her breath as if she had been holding it for a year.

AMONG THE buildings and the crowd, Timmy began to see familiar faces. Men in dark suits and white shirts and black suspenders nodded to his mother. Some of the men had twisted, corn picker hands. Women in long, dark dresses, their hair pulled tightly back, smiled at Timmy. From the hundreds of black shoes and boots, the ground between the buildings had been walked soft and slightly muddy, a mulch of dirt and grass and oak-leaf spines.

Ahead, the barn-sized, canvas sheets of the cook tent rippled from a breeze that Timmy could not feel. He kept looking around for Jacobsen, but did not see him. Timmy had a sudden fear that Jacobsen had not come this year, that he would be alone.

The parking-lot boy rapped on the wooden door of the cook tent marked OFFERINGS.

"Potatoes we need," a deep voice said. Big, white-shirted arms reached out for the sack. Timmy's mother steered him forward.

"Nice to see you again, Mrs. Gustafsen," the big man said to Timmy's mother. It was Garland Brown, one of the preachers, one of the Elders. He was taller than Timmy's father.

"And . . ." he looked down at Timmy.

"Timmy," his mother said. Her cheeks brightened with color.

"Yes, of course."

Behind Garland Brown, lit by a single bulb which dangled from a black cord, were tall pine shelves filled with jars of canned fruit and vegetables: pale pears, purple cherries, red tomato sauce, yellow string beans, green dill pickles, ruby-colored beet pickles, black jellies. On the ground, stacked high, were piles of pumpkins and squash, crates of red and yellow apples, and cardboard boxes of onions. The smells all mixed together sweet and sharp, like cold mincemeat pie or dill juice.

Garland Brown squinted past Timmy and his mother; the light bulb sent the shadow of his nose down onto the square of his jaw. "Just the two of you?" he said.

"I'm afraid so," Timmy's mother said. She looked down briefly.

"Don't be afraid," the big man said to Timmy's mother, "not here."

Timmy's mother nodded. She tried to smile. "Next year. Maybe next year he'll come," she said.

"That's better," Garland Brown said. "That's the spirit."

The color in her cheeks brightened further. Timmy thought of apples, Prairie Spy apples, and of his mother's brown hair rippling in the wind, flowing long and brown over his father's face and clear out the truck window into blue summer night.

"If you need anything, let me know," Garland Brown said. He swung their sack of potatoes on the pile behind.

Timmy's mother smiled gratefully, then turned away. Outside, they walked toward the women's dormitory.

Timmy kept looking for Jacobsen.

THEY REACHED the front door of the women's quarters at the same time as another woman and her daughter, who had yellow hair and who was exactly Timmy's size. Timmy and the girl stared at each other for a moment, then quickly looked away. Timmy's mother put her hand on his shoulder, letting the woman and her daughter go in first, then turned to him. She knelt down and looked at Timmy for a long moment. He looked away.

"Would you like to sleep in the men's quarters this year?" she asked.

"Alone?" Timmy asked quickly.

"No, no." She laughed. She hugged him. "Come on."

They waited by the wooden cook-tent door until Garland Brown reappeared.

"There is something," Timmy's mother said to him. She and Garland talked softly for a few moments.

Garland Brown came over to Timmy. "Well, we'd better get this young man a place to sleep—up in the men's building. I'm just about through here, in fact I could use a hand." He held out his hand, beckoned Timmy forward.

Timmy stepped forward, afraid but excited. His mother smiled. He was glad she did not hug him.

"Here are his things," she said.

THE MEN's dormitory was a long wooden building with plank floors and rows of straw ticks. Just as in the women's building, the first floor was for the older men, the second floor for the younger men. Timmy and Garland Brown climbed to the second floor. As Timmy was spreading out his bedroll on a tick next to Garland's, someone said loudly, "Say there, Gustafsen!"

Quickly Timmy turned around. At first he did not recognize the speaker, who looked somewhat like his old friend Jacobsen. But it had to be Jacobsen because behind him was Jacobsen's father. Last year Jacobsen had been only a little taller than Timmy. This year Jacobsen was as big as a man. Red pimples the size of pin cherries banded his neck, and there was a razor burn on his chin. Timmy jerked his head in recognition; Jacobsen had taught him to do that.

"See you at the first meeting!" Jacobsen said.

"Right," Timmy answered. He saw that Jacobsen carried a new black Bible. Jacobsen saw Timmy look at it, and put his other hand over its cover. Timmy stared. Jacobsen carrying a Bible?

"I'll save you a place," Jacobsen said.

LATER, STANDING in line by the main hall, Jacobsen said, "I figured we should get here early so we can get a seat right next to the back door, in case we have to vamoose." He grinned, but his grin did not come fully into his eyes. He did not explain the Bible, and Timmy didn't ask. They stood without speaking. Jacobsen scrubbed his chin with his knuckles so that his new whisker stubble made noise.

"So where's your old man?" Jacobsen asked.

Timmy was silent. "Didn't come," he said finally.

"You said he was comin' this year."

Timmy said nothing.

"Why doesn't he come?" Jacobsen asked.

"He doesn't believe in it," Timmy answered.

"In what?"

Timmy was quiet a moment. "In God."

"So what does he believe in?"

"Things," Timmy said.

"Like what?"

Timmy stared beyond Jacobsen. "Things. Like fence posts, hammers, and tractors."

Jacobsen nodded. "Your old man ain't so dumb," Jacobsen said, "nossir." But then he said to Timmy, "So what about you?"

"So what about me?" Timmy said. He had learned that from Jacobsen, too.

Jacobsen said, "Your mother believes in God, 'cause she's here, and your father believes in fence posts and hammers. What do you believe in?"

Timmy looked away. People around him and Jacobsen had turned to stare. He looked back to Jacobsen, then down to the dirt. To the damp grass.

TIMMY and Jacobsen sat in the back row of the hall. During the first sermon Jacobsen took notes. Timmy leaned over to see what he was writing, but Jacobsen kept it covered with his big hands. During the second sermon, Jacobsen tore off the page, put it into his Bible, and handed the Bible to Timmy. Timmy unfolded the paper. It was a drawing of a naked woman pointing to her crotch and of a scarecrow man holding out his big thing toward her. Timmy clapped shut the Bible. His neck turned hot. He looked up to see if people were turning to stare at him.

Jacobsen covered up his laughter by coughing loudly. Later he drew another picture, but this time added wavy motion lines behind the man's butt. Timmy stared straight ahead, trying to ignore Jacobsen. After a while Jacobsen seemed to forget about Timmy. Timmy sneaked a sidelong look. Jacobsen was listening to the sermon, his jaw slack, his forehead furrowed.

FOR THE NEXT two days, Timmy saw his mother only at meeting times. Jacobsen and some other boys and Timmy did everything together. He had not wanted to hang around with Jacobsen, but it was fun most of the time. Jacobsen was the leader. He knew all the secrets to the convention grounds, like where to find crab apples and how to get into the attic of the meeting hall. The group chased and played between every meeting and stayed out as late as they dared at night. But they never missed any meetings; Jacobsen made sure of that.

The evening of the third day there was a meeting for young people only. Two of the younger preachers asked questions about the Bible. Girls, and Jacobsen, knew all the answers.

"Abraham and Isaac!" shouted Jacobsen before anyone else. His bobbing throat worked his beard stubble as he waited for the next question.

"Gabriel!" Jacobsen answered triumphantly.

"That's very good," one of the preachers said, "but we must let the others have a turn."

Jacobsen tensed for the next question.

AFTER THE meeting Timmy asked Jacobsen how he knew all that Bible stuff. The question made Jacobsen stop walking. He stared at Timmy. His eyes were serious, and Timmy felt funny in their gaze. But then Jacobsen shrugged his shoulders.

"Aw, hell, you hear it around."

"Come on," Timmy said.

"I have a phonographic memory, I guess," Jacobsen said.

Timmy did not understand, but that didn't matter. There was still time to do something fun before the main meeting

that evening. "Come on," Timmy called to Jacobsen, "let's go
get some crab apples." Timmy started to run, but Jacobsen did
not follow. Timmy stopped.

"Come on, let's do something," he said to Jacobsen.

"We done everything," Jacobsen said.

Timmy was silent. Jacobsen had never said anything like
that before. They watched people file into the main meeting
hall.

"Garland Brown is preaching tonight," Jacobsen said. "I
figured I'd get a seat right up front. I mean it's just as easy
cuttin' out the front door as it is the back door," he quickly
added. "Hell, we should sit up front all the time. We could
really cut out of here fast that way, couldn't we?"

But Jacobsen's voice was funny, and his eyes were scared.
Timmy did not answer him.

GARLAND STEPPED to the microphone as the hymn faded. His
brown eyes swept the crowd, swept away the last rustling of
hymnals closing. In the silence he raised high his right hand,
then slowly drew it down, swimming his fingers in descent,
like something falling.

"And there was a shining in the air," he said softly, "and it
was the angel Gabriel."

Brown began slowly, speaking softly of the descent of Gabriel to earth and his Annunciation to the Virgin Mary of the
incarnation of Christ. He carried the microphone back and
forth across the stage, turning again and again to address himself to the deepest corners of the meeting hall. Soon Garland
Brown's face shone sweat, and he took off his coat.

"And there was a shining in the air," he repeated, beginning
to stalk the stage now, pointing into the crowd, chopping the
air with his hands.

"And there was a shining in the air, yes there was."

Timmy began to mouth the words in return, the words
about the shining. He repeated them again and again during
the long sermon until he knew when they would come around
again; he began to ride with them far out in Garland's story

of Gabriel. The words were a merry-go-round, circling, circling, and Timmy began to feel funny, dizzy. To clear his head, he pulled his eyes from Garland Brown and made himself stare at the concrete floor, at the crushed spears of grass, at the flecks of dried mud on his boots.

It was then Timmy noticed the smell. It was a sour smell, like silage, like a locker room. He turned to Jacobsen. Jacobsen's wool suit coat was black with wetness from armpit to waist. A clear droplet of sweat wavered down the inside of Jacobsen's wrist, then disappeared into his palm. Jacobsen's eyes were welded to the stage, to Garland Brown, and his slack lips mumbled after the preacher's words, "There was a shining in the air."

AFTER THE sermon, people crowded forward to shake hands with Garland Brown. Timmy threaded his way toward the main door. Jacobsen followed. The night air outside was chilly and smelled of damp dirt and leaves. Timmy breathed deeply. The cold air felt good; it was waking him up.

Jacobsen lingered in the shadow of the main door, saying nothing. Timmy leaned against the building with him. There were stars out, lots of them, and one fell even as he looked. He thought of the story of Gabriel. He turned to Jacobsen.

"See you later, then," Jacobsen said.

"Huh?" Timmy said.

"I said see you later. We're not hangin' out tonight," Jacobsen said.

"Why?"

"I can't."

"Why?"

"Because there's things I've got to do tonight," he said.

"What things?" Timmy asked.

"Things—and not kid things," Jacobsen said. "Now, get lost!"

Timmy walked away without looking back. He circled back, however, along the shadow of the cook tent and stood where he could watch Jacobsen. Jacobsen waited by the meeting-hall door, in the darkness. The stream of people coming out of the yellow-lit doorway began to thin. Then Garland Brown appeared. Jacobsen stepped forward into the light.

TIMMY LAY on his mattress in the dark with his eyes open. He wondered why Jacobsen had waited to see Garland Brown. And he wondered about the story of the angel Gabriel. He could not remember many of the words of the sermon now, except for the part about the shining, about Gabriel coming out of the clouds and the sunlight glinting off his wings. But now in the dark, the pictures of the angel that came to mind were not so large or so bright as before.

Suddenly Garland Brown was in front of his mattress, taking off his coat. Then his pants. His figure grew white and tall in his long underwear, then folded small as Garland Brown knelt beside his mattress. He put his hands to his forehead, murmured a short prayer, then crawled under his blankets. Straw crackled in the tick, then went silent. He let out a long breath. Faint moonlight shone in Garland Brown's eyes, then went out.

Timmy lay stiffly, afraid that Garland would hear his heart pounding. Suddenly Timmy heard his own voice blurt, "Is it true?"

"What's that?" Garland Brown said with a start.

Timmy was silent for a while. Then he whispered, "Is it . . . all true?"

"Son, is what true?" he said.

"Gabriel . . . that story."

Garland Brown drew in a breath. "You mean my sermon tonight?"

"Yes," Timmy said.

Garland was silent for a long time. He put his arms behind his head and looked into the darkness. Moonlight shone in his eyes again.

"Son," he said, his voice soft, "that's something you'll have to find out for yourself. That's the best way. And here, this will help you." He felt behind his bed for a few moments, then found a thin black book which he handed to Timmy. In the faint night light of the hall, Timmy saw it was a Bible, a Bible exactly like the one Jacobsen carried.

THE NEXT DAY was Sunday, the last day of church camp. All day Timmy carried the new Bible. It made him feel taller, older. Garland showed him the story of the angel Gabriel. Timmy read it over and over, even missing lunch before the last meeting in order to get a good seat in the main hall.

The last meeting of the camp was always special. At the end of the meeting there was profession for those who wished to join the faith of Garland Brown. People professed by standing during the last hymn and walking to the front of the hall where they turned to face the crowd.

Jacobsen was already seated when Timmy entered the hall. Timmy sat by him, but Jacobsen would not say anything or even look at him. He stared straight ahead and was sweating like the night before. His fingers left moons of wetness on his Bible, and when the hymns started, Jacobsen sang loudly, almost shouting the words.

By the second verse of the last hymn, several young people were standing and then moving down the aisles to the front. Their faces were shiny with tears. Jacobsen swallowed again and again. During the last verse he suddenly stood up and mounted the platform with the others. Tears streamed from Jacobsen's chin. He looked straight at Timmy, who could taste salt from his own tears. With a slow motion of his head, Jacobsen beckoned Timmy toward the front. Timmy felt himself moving, slipping forward on his chair. But at the last moment before he stood, someone big sat down in Jacobsen's empty chair and put a heavy arm around Timmy's shoulders. It was Garland Brown. He smiled down at Timmy. His arm pressed down gently on Timmy's shoulders and remained there until the meeting was over.

Back in the truck, Timmy and his mother were on the highway, headed home. His mother talked on about Jesus, God, and the disciples and all the wonders to be found in the Bible. Garland Brown had talked with her after the last meeting, had told her about Timmy's interest in the gospel. The big preacher had said that Timmy should read the Bible in the coming year, read it and think about it, and find out for himself if it was all true.

His mother talked on, excitedly. Timmy listened, planing his head against the warm wind of the September fields. Soon there were too many sons and fathers and brothers with long names to remember, and he knew Garland Brown was right. He had to find out for himself. He began to think hard about something Garland had told him.

Timmy had asked how he would know if the story of Gabriel and the Bible was true. And Garland told him that when he saw the truth and the light, something would happen. Something large and clear would happen and change everything.

Timmy began to watch the passing fields, the highway, the sky. He looked much longer at everything, longer and harder than usual, watching for . . . something. Something he had never noticed before. But the passing rows of corn blurred and spun backwards as always. The sparrow hawks sat nervously on the telephone wires, neither brighter nor quicker than before church camp. And the sky was the same high blue. Once, a farmer on a tractor levered up his plow at the fence just as their truck passed; for an instant the plowshares flashed like mirrors. But then the turn was completed, the plow cut back into the ground, going away. Timmy's heart came alive at the flashing—but it was over so quickly; there was only a man in the field, plowing.

BY THE TIME the truck passed through Groton, back into the prairie land, Timmy stopped staring at everything they passed. He had watched everything and had seen nothing. Nothing was different. Nothing had changed. There were no signs. And the strength of church camp and Garland Brown weakened every mile closer to home.

Ahead, their farm came into view. It, too, was the same. The barn, the windbreak, overhead some white jet trails. Timmy saw his father far out in the field, working on some fencing, and was suddenly excited to see him. His mother slowed the truck and honked. His father turned to look but did not wave. Timmy jumped out and began to run across the field toward his father.

Timmy was halfway to his father when he saw it. He stopped as though he had smashed into some invisible wall; far out in the field, in the sky above his father, something glinted. Something slowly drifting down from the sky, glinting, shining, shimmering. Timmy cried out and ran toward the shining. It was now nearly to the ground. He cried for his father to come and see.

Timmy knelt by it on the ground. It was a tangle of thin strips of aluminum foil, like tinsel that hung on a Christmas tree. He looked up—at the long, white jet trails—just as his father reached him.

"What did you say that was?" his father asked.

Timmy looked at the mass of foil and his mouth went dry.

"Angel feathers," Timmy whispered.

"Angel feathers," his father said. He laughed. "You been hearing too much preaching, I can see that. Radar—that's what it's for. The planes drop it to test their radar."

Timmy picked up the tangle of foil. His mother approached, still carrying her Bible. They watched her come. When she stopped, Timmy stood exactly halfway between his father and his mother.

"What's that? What have you found?" she asked, staring at the foil in Timmy's hand.

Timmy looked down at it again, then up to the high, blue, empty sky. He wadded the foil into a hard little ball and let it drop.

"Nothing," Timmy said, "it's nothing at all."

He stepped toward his father.

HEART OF THE FIELDS

THE HUNTERS were all Hansens. They were all dressed in red and stood in the snow near their pickups. Benny's father said again, "You're sure there was nothing."

"Nothing," Benny said.

Benny's father cursed; his breath smoked in the December air and a clear droplet spun from his nose.

Benny turned away. He leaned on his rifle and tried to get his breath without taking the frozen air too deeply into his lungs. Beside Benny, three of his cousins were lying back on the snow, their coats open at the throat and steaming. Benny and they had just finished driving the big timber where the snow was hip-deep in places. Benny's father, his uncles, and his grandfather had been on stands waiting for the deer to break out. There had been no deer.

Benny looked down the field to his grandfather. The grandfather's gray Ford sat parked in the northeast corner of the hay field, alongside a low patch of brush. The brush broke the outline of the Ford, shielded it from the timber and from the eyes of any deer that might try to come east across the open snow. A yard-wide oval of carbon blackened the snow beneath the Ford's tailpipe. To keep warm, his grandfather ran the motor all day. By its constancy, the Ford's dull, thumping idle was a part of the landscape of pines and snow and fields, a sound that, like a steady breeze, went unnoticed until it died. But during deer season, the Ford's pumping rhythm never ceased.

Benny wondered if his grandfather got lonely, there in the car all day. He knew his grandfather took with him only a cold egg sandwich, a thermos of Sanka, and the old twelve-gauge shotgun with a single slug—"In case one tries to come east," as the old man said every year.

The grandfather no longer carried his own deer rifle, the silvery Winchester Model 94. Benny had it. Benny's father and uncles decided those things. They awarded the rifle to Benny because they believed the grandfather's eyes were too dim to make good use of the rifle, and because, at age thirteen, Benny was the oldest grandchild.

Benny drew his glove along the worn walnut stock of the Winchester. He thought of walking on to the Ford to talk with his grandfather, but in the failing light the snowy road lengthened even as he watched. Today, however, was the last day of deer season. They would not have to hunt tomorrow, and Benny would visit him then. He would make lunch, scrambled eggs and toast and cranberry jelly and Sanka, for his grandfather. And then they would sit together by the oil burner and listen to the radio.

"Well—that's it for this year," Benny's father said, and cursed again.

Benny turned. Across the blueing snow, two fluorescent orange hunting caps swam out from the timber's shadow. Drawing light from air, the hats bobbed toward Benny and the others in separate rhythms. They were the last of the drivers. There was now no chance for deer.

"Weren't nothing in there," one of the cousins muttered from the snow.

"The hell," Benny's father said quickly, "there's deer tracks goin' into that timber but none comin' out. What does that tell you? It tells me you drivers got too spread out and the deer got back through you."

None of the drivers said anything because Benny's father was right. Some of the cousins, disoriented by the gray, sunless sky, had wandered in and out of the drive-line. Other cousins, tired of the deep snow, walked the higher ridge trails instead of working through the bottom brush in the draws and holes. The deer, a great buck along with some does, had not stirred.

Hell, maybe the deer weren't in the timber in the first place, Benny thought. Though he had seen the buck's tracks earlier in the day, had seen the buck himself in the alfalfa and cornfields all that fall, by now Benny barely believed in the gray-brown ghosts.

A hundred yards away, the orange caps rode bodies now, Benny's Uncle Karl and another cousin. "So where'd they go?" Karl called across the snow as if to get in the first word.

Benny's father spit.

"They didn't cross south," Karl continued, waving his rifle. "They didn't go west because of the lake. And they didn't come north because you were there. Unless you didn't see 'em."

"They didn't come north," Benny's father said, a tic of anger working his forehead.

The cousins were all standing now.

"Hell, I don't know," Karl muttered. "Maybe they're hiding under these goddamn pickups."

His boot thudded against the fender and snow fell over the tire.

"Maybe they came east, through here . . ." one of the cousins said.

"Then Grandpa would have seen them," Benny answered immediately.

The hunters all looked, first at Benny, and then down the field at the grandfather's Ford. They had forgotten the grandfather.

But Karl turned his back on the grandfather's car. "Hell, the way his eyes are these days, he couldn't see a deer if it jumped over his car."

Benny turned quickly to his father, who only looked down and kicked snow from his boots as he nodded in agreement.

"Honk the horn for him," Karl said, jerking his head toward the Ford, and, "let's go home."

"I will! I will!" Two of the youngest cousins scrambled to be the first into the pickups. The horns blared across the fields and their echoes wavered back from the timberline. The others began to case their rifles but Benny remained standing, angered at his father and uncle. He waited for the Ford's brake lights to blink on red, for the race of the engine and the black blossom of exhaust.

But the Ford's idle pulsed evenly on. There was no blink of light, no black smoke, nothing. From the side of his eye Benny saw his father, gun half cased, look up and freeze. The others straightened and stared downfield at the Ford. White-faced and wide-eyed, the cousins at the pickup horns now looked about as if they had done some terrible wrong.

"Honk again," Benny's father said with an old slowness.

The horns blared and the timber honked back the faded replies.

"Again," Karl said quickly.

At the third honking there was motion near the Ford, brown motion from the brush alongside the car. Three deer uncoiled from the bushes, their white tails flagged up and bouncing. Behind Benny someone scrambled for a rifle. "No—" Benny's father shouted.

The big buck and two does leaped a car's length in front of the Ford and then ran straight away north. The buck's antlers flashed through a last slant of sunlight and then all three deer disappeared into the shadow of the timber.

"Holy Christ—" someone began, but stopped. In the silence, the Ford's thumping idle beat in the air like the heart of the fields.

"Grandpa!" Benny cried. He ran toward the Ford, tearing off his coat for speed, outdistancing the others. As he neared the car he saw his grandfather slumped in the front seat. Benny tore open the door.

"What? Whoa!" his grandfather exclaimed with a start. "You scared me there, Benny!"

"Grandpa! Are you—didn't you hear us honk?"

The grandfather blinked. The white wisps of his eyebrows moved as he thought. "I don't rightly know," he finally said. "I guess I heard, but then I thought I was dreaming. Or something like that. I wasn't sleeping, nossir. But I was dreaming, somehow . . ." His voice trailed off. The others were there now, crowding around the car. Benny held on to his grandfather. He buried his face in the roughness and the woody smell of the old wool coat and held his grandfather tight.

"Here now, Benny," the old man said, "where's your coat? It ain't July."

One of the cousins had retrieved Benny's coat, and he stood up to put it on. His grandfather squinted around at the hunters. "Any luck today, boys?" he said.

No one said anything. Then Benny's father said, "No, no luck today, Dad."

The grandfather shook his head. "Guess we'll have to eat track soup this year. And that's thin eating, I always said."

Benny's father nodded.

"Everybody's out?" the grandfather asked, peering across to the timber he could not see.

"Everybody's out," Karl answered.

"I'll drive on home then, and get myself a hot cup of Sanka."

The Ford's engine raced briefly, then the car lurched forward; on the snow was a dark rectangle of wet leaves and grass. The Ford receded up the snowy field-road toward the yellow yard-light and buildings. The hunters stared after him. "I'll be damned," one of the men murmured.

Karl turned away to inspect the deer beds, three gray ovals in the snow, and beside them the scuffed hearts of the leaping hooves. But darkness had fallen and the hunters soon pressed on to their pickups.

Benny's father led the caravan. He drove in the grandfather's tracks that led up to the old house and then beyond, to the country road that forked away to their own farms and homes.

But tonight the chain of headlights behind Benny and his father did not pass through the grandfather's yard. One by one the trucks turned in and parked. Doors thudded. Laughter hung in the frosty air as the Hansens, all of them, converged on the yellow lights of the grandfather's house.

THE BREAD-TRUCK DRIVER

JERRY LEE SPANGLER woke up hard. He'd been dreaming of the college professor, the one on his bread route. She was sunning herself on a wooden dock, lying naked on her stomach on the hot pine boards. Jerry Lee was a fish in the water below. He darted through the cold water, finning back and forth through slats of sunlight and shadow, the long white cloud of her body floating just above him. Her eyes were closed. She lay baking in the heat just out of reach.

Jerry Lee blinked and turned to the bedside clock. Its blue glow read "TODAY." He squinted and leaned closer. This time it read 4:00 AM.

Jerry Lee lay back and smiled.

The dream.

Then the clock.

He believed in signs, and the signs said today. Today was the day he would make his move on Professor Leslie Feinstein.

Beside him, Jerry Lee's wife snored on. She lay on her side, back to Jerry. He ran his hand over the big curve of her hips. From having kids, six of them, his wife's rear was big as a truck tire, but in the dark she still felt good. All women did. Jerry Lee thought briefly of slipping up her nightgown and sliding into her. She wouldn't mind. She'd wake up slow and brace

her legs to push back against him, and afterwards fall asleep
again without a word, her nightgown still hoisted. But Jerry
Lee had to piss, and besides, it was Monday.

Monday was Jerry Lee's long route, north on Highway 64
through the farm towns, then east on County 86, a snake's
trail of yellow gravel that curved around blue lakes. After
gravel he drove on pine needles down the narrow, tree-shaded
driveways to the resorts, to their little grocery stores whose
wire racks twice a week he filled with bread. Resorts like
Whispering Pines, where the Feinsteins lived.

Two squirrels slammed onto the roof. Leslie Feinstein jerked
upright in bed as the squirrels galloped up the shingles, skit-
tered over the tin ridge roll, then drummed down the other
side.

Her heart hammered. The little bastards!

She turned to Ethan, her husband. Sleeping on his side, his
back to her, Ethan breathed on. His snore was a sound like
salt water tumbling onto shore, falling silent for a moment
at its high water mark, then sliding with a hiss down a long
gravelly slope.

How could he not have heard the squirrels?

How was that possible?

She lay back. The depth, the heaviness, of Ethan's sleep had
always irritated her, an objection which if she were honest she
would admit was connected to his size. He was six foot four
and weighed two hundred twenty-some pounds. He was per-
sonally responsible for neither, certainly not his height, but in
marriage, nothing excused anything. In bed Ethan's back and
shoulders rose like a great cliff; land's end. On campus full
Professor Ethan Feinstein loomed similarly large in his tweed
coats (46 XL) and thick-weave turtlenecks, a sturdy figure
around whom women graduate students tended to cluster.
Even Leslie's women friends admired the sheer bulk of Ethan.
Often they made sly jokes about the size of his hands, the
length of his fingers. But of course none of them had to sleep
with him.

(Or did they? Had they? How many?)

Her heart still thumping lightly, Leslie stared at the pine knots in the ceiling.

Monday. July 10. The Year of Our Lordly Resort Experiment.

One checkout, cabin four, a couple in their early thirties, without children, who came out only onto the porch of their cabin and then only at sundown.

Rake the beach (wet pine needles, lily-pad leaves).

Check the gas tank in the boat house; call if twenty gallons or less.

Life jackets in every boat?

She turned to Ethan's back. She stared for a moment at the furry cloak of hair that grew across his shoulders. She closed her eyes and summoned up *The Life and Times of Leslie Feinstein,* a documentary film she screened privately whenever the presence of Ethan loomed overly large. Leslie, too, was an English professor. Really.

She, too, was on a leave of absence from the University of Chicago. Really.

She, too, was a writer. She was working (intermittently) on a lengthy critical article (perhaps even a book) on Kate Chopin, a neglected American writer who had died in 1904; Leslie was proving a case of literary sabotage against Chopin, perpetrated by Henry James and William Dean Howells, who had conspired, she believed, to ruin Chopin's literary reputation through a pogrom of dignified silence.

Leslie opened her eyes. She tried to remember the last sentence she had written on her article. Had she left off with Howells? Or was it with James? She waited, staring at a particularly dark and swirling pine knot on the ceiling. Somewhere in the room a mosquito hummed.

Monday.

Some other Monday task buzzed in the periphery of her memory ("drummed like a woodpecker on the hollow log of my memory," her freshmen students might have written).

She missed her students.

Their kindly, dumb faces.

Their goofy, fumbled comments in class.

Their intensely personal essays wherein they wrote about first dates, lost loves, getting drunk, an abortion, a bad father, a kind teacher.

But Monday.

Oh yes, Monday.

Monday was bread day.

JERRY LEE SPANGLER hummed as he shaved, and thought about Leslie Feinstein. And her husband. Both were professors of some sort. They had come here to northern Wisconsin from Illinois. In Chicago they'd taught at some university.

No kids.

Late thirties, early forties.

All this Jerry had gotten from neighboring resorters. Leslie Feinstein herself never had much to say, and neither did her husband. Jerry Lee had only seen him once, a big, thick fellow with a gray beard. Not that Jerry worried about him, or about husbands in general.

That was the great part about being a bread-truck driver. When a woman knew what she wanted, and what she wanted was a half hour with Jerry Lee Spangler, there was never any husband problem. Whether she wanted Jerry Lee for thirty minutes on a piece of carpet padding on the cool concrete floor of the storeroom, eye level with the plastic bottles of liquid soaps and cleaning fluids that pushed sweet smells through the white and pink and yellow curves of their bodies, or whether she wanted Jerry Lee for fifteen minutes inside a tin-roofed, heat-baked shed at lakeside on a pile of orange life jackets and boat cushions thrown down on the floor among Evinrude propellors and squat red fuel cans whose sweet gasoline breath wafted up the stud walls of rusty nails hung with minnow nets and cane poles and Dare-Devils, and far up in the peak the hornet's nest that hummed louder and louder the more commotion there was at floor level—or whether she wanted Jerry Lee for ten minutes inside his bread truck, in the narrow alley between

the racks of caramel rolls and apple Danishes and loaves of
white bread and packages of glazed doughnuts, on the hard
and warm maple floor with its sifting of bread crumbs and
sugar—if that's what she wanted, there was no husband problem. Women took care of their husbands. Jerry took care of
the wives.

Jerry Lee whistled parts of "Blue Hawaii" in the shower, then
toweled off before the mirror. Leaning close to the steamed
glass, Jerry took his time shaving. He trimmed his dark brown
mustache, whose color matched his eyes. He clipped a couple
of stray eyebrow hairs, then surveyed himself in the mirror.
Since he didn't work outside, Jerry Lee had no farmer's
squint, no weathered creases around the eyes and mouth; his
face was smooth and open. A trustworthy face. Jerry had a
full head of walnut brown hair (once a week he used a few
drops of Walnut Brown Herculean Formula Touch-up from
a small bottle which he kept below the basin, behind the Liquid Drano bottle). He kept his hair slightly longer in the
front and on top; the sides he combed back. Jerry Lee wore
his hair now the same way he had worn it in high school but
without the grease—like Elvis in his Las Vegas phase. Jerry
Lee narrowed his eyes as he gave his hair a quick misting
with his wife's hairspray. He counted to thirty, then shook his
head lightly. Nothing moved.

Jerry Lee stepped back from the mirror. He flexed his
arms. Hauling racks of bread continually for the past fifteen
years, though they weren't heavy, had given him the muscle
tone of an eighteen-year-old. He put on deodorant, patted Old
Spice Men's Talcum down his chest and into his pubic hair,
put on a freshly pressed, tan-colored pair of short-sleeved
coveralls that read "Jerry" above the left pocket and "Sunny-
Style" above the right. He carefully rolled up both shirtsleeves
to show the sharp ridge of his triceps. Lastly he slid into a
fresh pair of white cotton socks, his crepe-soled black shoes,
then slipped from the house into the purple July morning.

There were no other lights in his neighborhood of trailer
homes. He had a double-wide thirty-six-foot RolloAir with

a dish on top. Jerry Lee had long ago quit crawling underneath the trailer to check the condition of its tires. Fifteen
years with SunnyStyle, no crack-ups, no boozing, always on
time—friendly, well-groomed Jerry Lee wasn't going anywhere.

He thought of Leslie Feinstein. He wondered why she'd
left the university. A good government job like that, all those
benefits. He'd once heard a teacher's joke about the three main
benefits of the job: June, July, and August.

He thought more.

People gave things up for a reason.

They were unhappy.

They wanted something.

Something more.

Something better.

Which translated to Somebody.

Jerry Lee checked his hair in the mirror.

LESLIE FEINSTEIN, lying absolutely still beside snoring Ethan,
her hand beneath the covers, beneath the elastic band of her
panties, was finding her stride, nearing the home stretch of an
intensely personal hand race (she had long ago run track and
remembered the springiness of rubberized asphalt, the smell of
liniment and discarded ankle tapes heating in the sun, the in-
credible lightness of track shoes with their leather cut low below the ankle bone, the string bikini of shoes, how they made
the legs feel longer; she remembered the bend of the legs, the
white calves that the runners flexed and shook, then drew up
hard as they tensed before starting blocks), and now, here in
bed, nearing her own finish line, the boys' and then men's
faces began to lope through her mind—any face that had ever
caught her attention remained with her forever—they all came
on fast at the finish line, racing toward her, a dark-haired janitor from grade school, her high school track coach, her own
father, her uncle Ned, her track coach, her father again, a
Mexican boat-boy from Acapulco, the black-haired janitor
again, the bread-truck driver with his funny hair, all closing
on her with increasing speed, jostling each other, trying to

reach her at exactly the Right Moment, to be The One (and
it was always a different One—never Ethan) depending how
fast and how long she made them run, how badly they—

When someone pounded on the door.

Leslie jerked away her hand.

Ethan snorted and rolled onto his stomach.

She waited, heart beating hard. The door rattled again beneath someone's fist.

Leslie pulled on jeans and sweatshirt. She peered out the
kitchen window, which was low and open to the screen. On
the porch, fishing poles in hands, tackle boxes in the other,
pregnant in orange life jackets, was cabin five, the white-
haired couple from Indiana.

"Yes?" Leslie said. She brushed back her hair.

"There aren't any night crawlers in the refrigerator," the
wife said.

Leslie stared.

"The refrigerator in the boat house," the husband added.
He smiled. He had false teeth, the kind that turned milky
along the gums.

"We planned to go bass fishing this morning but there ain't
any crawlers," the wife said. She wore a raincoat beneath the
life jacket.

"I . . . haven't been to town," Leslie said.

"Every year we've been here, there's been crawlers in the
refrigerator," the woman said.

"I'll try to get to town this afternoon," Leslie said.

"Wouldn't have to," the husband said brightly. "You can
dig crawlers right here. When Bill Jenkins owned this place
he aways dug them over behind cabin three." He pointed his
arm.

Leslie stared. She turned to the wife. "Then why can't you
dig some for this morning? There's a shovel in the boat house."

"We didn't pay to come here and dig crawlers," the woman
said.

"What did you come here for?" Leslie said.

"Mabel—" the man said to his wife.

"For . . . service."

"So serve yourself," Leslie said. "It's six o'clock in the god-damn morning." She slammed the door.

"Les . . . who . . . what was that?" Ethan mumbled from the bedroom.

"President Reagan. And Nancy."

"Good. . . ," Ethan said. "Are they . . . coming back?"

"We hope not," Leslie said.

"Right. . . ," Ethan said. The bedroom fell silent again.

Leslie turned to the kitchen, to the coffeepot. She was putting the filter together when a fat shadow fell through the kitchen window. The woman from Indiana said through the screen, "This resort has never been so shabby. We've been coming here for thirty years and this is the first year the lawn isn't even fully raked—"

"So grab a goddam rake," Leslie shouted. "And a paintbrush and a hammer and a shovel, instead of sitting around like a fat old toad on a stump!"

"Hey," Ethan called. He stumbled into the kitchen. No shirt, big belly hanging over his jeans, cock half tumescent. "Steady here. Containment, Leslie, that's what we need here."

"I'm sorry," Ethan said to the woman, steering Leslie to the side, "my wife is not . . . a morning person, if you know what I mean."

The woman stared at Ethan, at his belly.

"There's no crawlers," she said.

"No crawlers is not a problem," Ethan said. "I'll get you some crawlers."

The woman looked up. "And there's no bread in the store, either. Not one slice," the woman said.

"No bread," Ethan said. He turned to Leslie. "Why is there no bread?"

"No night crawlers and no bread," the woman said. "What kind of resort is this?"

"The last," Leslie said.

Ethan went outside and led the woman down the path into a

patch of early sunlight. Leslie fitted the coffeepot together. Ethan spoke with the woman for several minutes. He smiled and gestured once. The woman nodded. She laughed briefly, then turned to glower again at the kitchen window.

Leslie made toast. She smeared peanut butter and honey on the toast. She heard Ethan chuckle. The woman laughed once, too, more of a rusty cackle than a laugh.

Soon Ethan came back through the door. "What the hell are you trying to do?" he said.

Leslie chewed her honey toast.

"You want everybody to go away?" he said.

"Sounds fine to me," she said.

Ethan stared at her for long moments, his hands on his hips. Her heart began to beat faster; she realized she had always been slightly afraid of him.

"Look," he said, "the plan was, we break away from school, come to some place like this for a couple years, get some writing done, then go back. And we will go back."

"Back to your grad students? And my women friends, all big fans of yours?"

"Lay off," Ethan said, "we've been through that." He turned away to the coffeepot. He poured a cup, then went to the toaster. There was one slice, a crust, left in the bread sack. He turned to Leslie. "Is there more bread?" he said.

"Yes," Leslie said. She held up the last bite of her toast, gave him a good look at it, then popped it into her mouth.

JERRY LEE's stepvan was third in line at the loading dock, so he walked inside the bakery. The warm breath of bread rolled over him. Mixer motors growled against their dough, the paddles turning with a steady hum and thump. Steel pans clanged here and there. Timers buzzed. Oven doors slammed. Radios played, some country music, some rock.

On his way to the coffee room Jerry Lee swung through the sweet-roll area and speared a fat, sugar-coated Bismarck jelly doughnut from the conveyer belt.

"Quarter!" called Shirley Hoffman, a thick-bodied middle-aged woman with a slight German accent and with hair tied up in a white kerchief. "You owe me!"

Jerry patted his pockets in sudden, mock concern. "Sorry," he said. "How about tomorrow?"

It was their regular conversation. He liked dependable things.

"Tomorrow, tomorrow—fifteen years' worth of tomorrow," Shirley said. "One Bismarck a day for fifteen years, you owe me anyway a thousand dollars."

"One night with me, I'm all paid up," Jerry said.

Still looking at Jerry Lee, Shirley spun a clear sheet of plastic wrap around her wrist, snapped it across fine metal teeth to cut it free, sheeted a tray of apple strudel so tight a dropped penny would bounce up and put out an eye. "One night with Elvis maybe," she said, "not you."

"Elvis is dead but I ain't," Jerry said. He kissed the jelly hole of the Bismarck with a loud smack.

Shirley grinned and shook her head. "Jerry Lee Spangler, I swear you get worse every year. And say—why aren't you on the road by now?"

"I'm gone," Jerry Lee said.

HE DROVE up Highway 64, making his regular stops in Farmington, Lakeside, Johnsville, Holdingtown, small farm towns with more and more of their main street windows blanked with plywood. Only the food stores never went belly up. People needed bread and milk. People had to eat.

In Belle Plains, the store owner's wife, Ida Mae, followed Jerry Lee outside to the truck. She was late forties, blond hair turning to gray, short, somewhat squat, with her legs starting to bulge with lumps like irregular loaves of bread. The kind no one will buy, the kind Jerry Lee got to take home and eat for free. As Ida Mae signed the bread ticket, her eyes watching her own pen move, she whispered, "Fred's going bass fishing all day next Thursday."

Her voice sounded funny, nervous and shaky, like it was short on air.

Women.

Jerry Lee loved them. When the women asked, that's when Jerry Lee loved them most of all. It took something to ask. It took something extra. Not many people had what it took to ask.

"You women," Jerry Lee said, clucking his tongue as he tore off the top page and fit the carbon carefully between the next two clean pages, "I don't know about you women." He reached for a mint-flavored toothpick from the cupful on his dashboard.

Ida Mae glanced briefly back to the side door, then turned to Jerry. "Well?" she said quickly.

"Thursday? Depends," Jerry Lee said. He rolled the toothpick from one side of his mouth to the other.

"On what?" Ida Mae said. Her eyes flickered again to the door.

"On if'd be worth my while."

"You damn well had fun last time," Ida Mae said. She set her lips.

"Sure enough—I'm not denying that," Jerry said, rolling his toothpick again. "But that was last week, today is today, and Thursday is four days away."

She waited.

"I need something to keep my mind occupied," Jerry Lee said. "Something to look forward to."

A loud car passed; Ida Mae glanced toward the street.

"Call it a preview," Jerry Lee said.

Ida Mae swallowed. "There's a closet," she said. Her cheeks colored and her voice went husky. "It's a broom closet inside the lady's bathroom. There's a slatted door you can see out, can't nobody see in."

"There you go," Jerry Lee said with a grin. "Now was that so hard?"

LESLIE FEINSTEIN stripped the sheets in cabin four, the young couple from Minneapolis. Something flew across the floor—a mouse—and lay dead in the corner.

Not a mouse, a damned condom.

Pigs. Not even the courtesy to flush their condoms down the toilet.

Then again condoms, like tampons, were death on septic systems (what the world needed was biodegradable condoms, though she could see several problems with such an invention, problems, of course, for women). She found a spoon in the kitchen, and with it pushed the dead, leaky mouse into the dustpan.

"Quite a bellyful on you, buddy," she muttered.

Then from her hands and knees she noticed an entire family of rubber mice peeking from beneath the bed.

She rolled away the bed. She counted.

Seventeen. Mother of Mary. Mouse family of seventeen flattened by Steamroller of Love. As she stared at the wet litter Leslie realized the man and the woman were, of course, each married to someone else. She swept away their evidence, and turned to the rest of the cabin.

The bathroom needed work.

The kitchen appeared untouched by human hands. What had they eaten? How had they kept their strength?

Finally she gathered the sheets. There were stains. Colors. Pale yellows, faint browns, one thin feather of red. At arm's length she quickly wadded the sheets and dropped them into the laundry basket. In the basket the sheets slowly uncoiled, blooming into curves, into shapes, shifting, turning into each other. Leslie paused to stare. When the sheets had stilled themselves she leaned closer, uncertain that they did not have a life of their own. Through the plastic grid of the laundry basket she smelled their perfume. Their coconut oil. Their fainter, earthier odors like petunias. Like geraniums in fresh dirt. Like a litter of young pups in a nest of rags.

Leslie took fresh sheets from the hamper, billowed the bottom sheet over the mattress, tucked the corners tightly. A fresh white canvas for the next artists of love. When she had finished, she paused to look out the window and down to the lake. Sunlight glittered on blue water. A few mothers sat in

beach chairs. Children dug in the sand. She wondered if the
lovers had looked out the window. Often? At all?

She stared at the water for a long time. Two small children
sat laughing in the wet sand; their mothers, one in a red suit,
the other in black, lay on towels, sunglassed eyes to the sky.
Music played faintly. As Leslie watched, the mother in the red
suit reached out and felt for her radio. Elvis's voice, some slow,
sad song, came up from the beach. Leslie listened but could
not catch the melody. The name. In the middle of the song she
turned away from the window and looked about the cabin. It
was hot and still. A cricket chirped once. Somewhere outside
a cicada buzzed. She went to the door, hooked its lock. Then
she went to the bed, turned back the clean sheets, took off her
clothes and lay down.

ON THE ROAD Jerry Lee listened to Elvis sing "Love Me Ten-
der." He knew all the words. When the song was over and
some news came on, Jerry Lee rolled the dial. The news made
people nervous, was Jerry's feeling. Floods. Airplane crashes.
Global warming. The ozone layer. AIDS. Everything in the
world was probably pretty much like it always had been, only
now there was more news so it was easier to get nervous about
things. That was Jerry's philosophy. People were here in this
world for a short enough time as it was.

He thought about Leslie Feinstein. Her quick brown eyes.
Edgy eyes, like there was something going on in the next room
that she'd just come from that she wasn't finished with. Leslie
Feinstein needed to relax more. She needed the full treatment,
mind and body, from Jerry Lee Spangler.

He should have been a professor. Some kind of doctor.

Jerry Lee Spangler: Doctor of Bread, Doctor of Love.

He turned down the narrow road with its tall dusty pines,
toward Whispering Pines, where Leslie lived. At the last bend
in the road before the resort, he stopped the stepvan, checked
his hair and took a small spray of breath deodorant. Then,
humming, he drove forward.

The Feinsteins' resort was nothing special, seven or eight small white wooden cabins that needed painting. The main office stood at the side of the largest cabin, which was where the Feinsteins lived. The little store, self-serve and always open, was attached to the office. Beyond the cabins were birch trees and patches of blue water.

Jerry Lee went into the office. It was empty but for a deerfly bumping against a window screen. Not even a radio playing. Jerry Lee rang the little bell and arranged himself at the counter.

A screen door slammed. Through the window he saw Leslie Feinstein come quickly from cabin four. She carried a laundry basket and walked fast. She was wearing faded jeans and a baggy white T-shirt. As she came closer he saw she was without a bra. Her tits were small and pointy, the kind that didn't fall with age, the kind that held steady as she walked, like headlights on high beam.

Jerry Lee crossed his legs, left one elbow on the counter.

In she came. Her dark hair, with just a touch of gray, was tied back in a ponytail; several strands dangled down the sides of her face.

"Howdy-doody," Jerry said.

"Hello there," she said, brushing back her hair. There was color in her cheeks and neck, like she'd been running or exercising. Her eyes flickered to the laundry basket, then back up.

"Laundry day?" Jerry Lee said.

"Every day's laundry day," she said. She turned and set the basket of sheets behind the counter.

"And Monday's bread day," Jerry Lee said.

Without speaking she walked toward the empty rack.

Jerry followed her. She had long legs. Jerry Lee imagined them knotted around his head.

"I was going to make a list," she said, staring at the empty wires.

"So let's make one together," Jerry Lee answered.

He stepped closer, produced his pad and a short pencil from inside the spiral ring. She was taller than him, and he was close

enough to smell Lysol and laundry soap on her hands. His cock
stirred inside his pants.

"Ready," he said.

"Eighteen white bread," she said.

"Eighteen white," Jerry said.

"Twelve whole wheat."

"Twelve whole," Jerry said.

"Ten bags of hamburger buns."

"Ten burger—regular or sliced?"

"Sliced."

"Sliced," Jerry said.

"Ten bags of hot-dog buns, sliced," she said.

"Ten dogs, sliced," Jerry said.

She paused.

"Any doughnuts, jelly-rolls, Mini-Apple Pies, shortcakes?"
Jerry Lee asked.

She thought a moment. "Three dozen doughnuts, a dozen
shortcakes." She paused, then turned to him. "Do you have
bagels?"

"Bagels?" he said. He thought a moment, frowning. "Bagels."

"They're . . . like doughnuts," she said.

"Don't think I've ever had bagels," Jerry Lee said.

"They're like doughnuts only they're harder and flatter,"
she added.

Jerry Lee shook his head no.

"They're harder and flatter and sometimes they have bits of
onion in them."

"I could special order—" Jerry began.

"They have a shiny glaze crust on top and you cut them in
half and eat them with cream cheese—" She had turned to
Jerry and drew bagel pictures with her hands. And she was
also starting to cry.

"Easy," Jerry Lee said, "I know a woman at the bakery,
Shirley," Jerry Lee said, "she'll know about bagels—"

"Or lox or just plain jelly or honey," she said.

Her voice had choked up to nothing and water ran from the
corners of her eyes.

"Hey, hey," Jerry Lee said. He reached out to touch her shoulder. She just stood there, crying. "Take it easy now," Jerry Lee said. He put his other hand on her other shoulder. "No tears," he said. He drew her closer to him until his arms were around her. A friendly hug, like people did on TV. "Listen," he said—her hair needed washing; he could smell its oil, which made his cock move—"listen, I know you get lonely out here. Everybody gets lonely, you get lonely, I get lonely on the road, everybody gets lonely, and there's no reason for that, because I want to tell you that you're the prettiest woman I seen in a long time and I think about you a lot . . ."

Leslie Feinstein looked up. Her mouth came open; her eyes widened and she pushed herself away from him.

"You came out here from the city, I know that's lonely. I also know that lonely is different for a woman than lonely is for a man—I'm one of the few men that thinks that way—and what I also think about is when your husband is gone sometime that you and me should find an empty cabin or take a blanket out into some secret spot you know in the woods, just you and me, Jerry Lee."

His heart drummed; he loved this moment. This moment was better, sometimes, than the real thing.

Leslie Feinstein's mouth hung open, then closed once or twice, but no words came out.

"I'm not pressing you," Jerry continued. "Probably today wouldn't work for you because these things take some planning, but I wanted you to know how I feel and that any time you want me, Jerry Lee's your man."

"I don't believe this," she murmured.

"Everything I said is true, and more," Jerry Lee began.

"The bread-truck driver," she said.

"That's me," Jerry said. "I deliver bread and I deliver anything else a woman needs."

"Whatever gave you the idea . . ." she began. Her eyes flickered down her T-shirt, her jeans, her tennis shoes, then came back to his.

"Clothes don't mean nothing to me," Jerry Lee said immediately. "Every woman's beautiful in her particular way. Maybe not all of her. But parts of her, yes. Every woman's got her own beauty, is the way I see it."

"See it?" she said faintly.

"I see different things in every woman," Jerry Lee said.

"In me, what possibly—" she began.

"I see you're at that age—thirty-eight, maybe more—when you don't know what to think of yourself," Jerry answered. "You're not young. You're not old. You're not sure how you look or who you are. You don't know if you can still get a man if you had to or if you wanted to, but I'm giving it to you straight, I'm telling you you can, and I want you to think over what I told you for a couple of minutes while I go get your bread, which won't take me long, which is correct, because some things should not be thought about too long, just like you can't bake a loaf of bread too long because it will dry up and be no good to anyone."

The bread-truck driver went through the door. Outside, Leslie heard the truck door rattle up, and, soon, the rolling crunch of little wheels on gravel. Leslie blinked. Quickly she got behind the counter. In another moment he came in, wheeling a blue car full of plastic trays of bread and rolls.

He grinned at her.

Leslie swallowed. "I should call your supervisor," she said.

"That's me," Jerry Lee said. "Bread-truck drivers are pretty much on their own." He turned to his bread, counting the loaves with one finger.

"Then I should throw you the hell out of here," Leslie said.

"Maybe so," Jerry said, still not looking at her. He began to toss the loaves like playing cards, each one loaf exactly beside the other, a hand of solitaire, onto the rack. "Maybe you're right," he said, glancing at her without slowing his motion, "but think about this. I'm polite and I'm clean," he said, "probably cleaner than most men you meet. I take my time in bed—what you like, I like. I don't tell—can't tell—because I don't know anybody that you know. And I'm not the worst-looking guy in the world."

Her eyes ran their quick gaze up and down the bread-truck driver.

He paused, one loaf of bread left in his hand. It was a longer, darker loaf. "Here," he said, "I had this in the truck. No bagels, but I thought you might like this."

He held out the loaf. "Rye, special order, unsliced," he said. "It's irregular, but so what."

She stared at the loaf. One side of it bulged, a loaf pregnant with another.

"It's on the house," he said. "On me, Jerry Lee."

She stared at the bread. Its bag was clouded from the inside like the steamed-up windows of a car. Bread breathing inside its bag.

"I was saving this loaf for myself," Jerry Lee said, "but I want you to have it."

He stepped closer and lay the loaf on the glass counter.

She could smell cologne. Fresh cologne. He had put on fresh cologne when he went to his truck for the bread.

"Try some," Jerry Lee said. He opened the plastic and slid out the loaf. On the glass counter, with a penknife, he slit the loaf across the middle. Broke it open. He cut a chunk from the very center of the loaf, impaled it on the little knife blade, and held it out to her. Dark brown rye bread. She could smell the grain.

"Go on," he said.

The bread jiggled in its freshness.

Leslie swallowed.

Suddenly she jerked backwards as if the bread were poison. "Who the hell are you, anyway? Who do you think you are?"

Jerry Lee drew back. He stared at the bread, then at her. His face was round-eyed, slightly hurt, puzzled. Then his face reclaimed itself, fell slowly back into a grin. "I'm the bread-truck driver. No more, no less."

"So how the hell can you go around"—Leslie ran her eyes from his ridiculous Elvis hair, his tight shirt, the rolled-up sleeves, the sharply ironed pants, the shiny black crepe-soled shoes, back to his unceasing grin—"thinking you're . . . somebody?"

"Oh, I know I'm somebody," Jerry Lee said. He pocketed his little notepad, glanced once around to make sure he had everything, then turned toward the door where he paused. "I got a job where people depend on me and I never let them down. I take a little fun along the way, and what's important, I give a little back, too. I sleep all night and I never have a bad dream," Jerry Lee said, "and that's because I know exactly who I am. The bread-truck driver."

He grinned once more, then wheeled his cart through the doorway. He leaned his head back through. "See you next Monday," he said, "same time, same station." He let his eyes flicker down Leslie once more, nodded appreciatively, and was gone.

"Get out of here—" Leslie shouted, too late. She grabbed the broken loaf of rye. "And take your damned irregular bread with you!"

LESLIE STOOD in the driveway and watched the bread truck disappear. Her heart pounded. Dust in the sunlight slowly settled in the trees, drifting down through pine needles and aspen leaves, back to the road where the bread she had thrown lay broken and scattered. She kicked at the bread, then turned back to the office. She sat on the stone steps for a long time. As the sunlight cleared itself of dust, so gradually did her mind.

She saw three possible endings to this . . . event? incident?

First, she would go immediately to Ethan and tell him about the bread-truck driver. Ethan would, momentarily, be angry at the interruption. Then engaged by her story. Then he would laugh, a long, wheezing, coughing, eye-watering fit of laughter. Which would make Leslie angry. Gradually aware of his rudeness, Ethan would turn solicitous. That night he would make dinner, a big chef's salad, and later, in bed, affirm his tenderness by holding her for quite a while before he gradually slid his hand between her legs.

In the second, more unlikely ending, Leslie would say yes to the bread-truck driver. Toward the end of the summer she would meet him in cabin three, they would have a couple of drinks, undress, and fall onto the bed, after which, in a loose manner of speaking, she would have had an affair. But this ending was even more unlikely than her telling Ethan. For by imagining Jerry Lee Spangler on top of her, his tight white butt rising and falling between her legs like a baker's fist punching dough, watching him accelerate, faster and faster, hitting harder and harder (she caught glimpses of herself falling into the rhythm, rising to meet him) until suddenly the whole action collapsed on top of her—by seeing all this play, filmlike, through some theater in her mind, Leslie also saw its true ridiculousness. Saw how small and absurd this event was in the full context of her life. Saw, in short, how the memory of it was not worth the risk of the real event.

Which was sad.

Which was a cool, detached, terribly sad way of looking at life.

The third ending seemed more likely. It was an ending composed of nothing. She would say nothing. She would do nothing, neither with the bread-truck driver nor with Ethan. Things would go on as they were. She would remain with Ethan at the resort, rake leaves and clean cabins and write intermittently, and finally go back to Chicago where she would think, on occasion, and always with a brief laugh, about the time the bread-truck driver tried to seduce her.

This ending seemed most likely because it entailed no risk yet still left her with the memory. It was not, of course, a memory of an afternoon in a sun-baked lake cabin with a bread-truck driver—but a memory close enough to the real thing that she might, years later, having wondered about it often, be unsurprised to find it changing shape. She could imagine, with time, the incident slowly reforming, expanding, swelling beyond the boundaries of its true body. She could foresee, many years later, the scattered bread and settling dust of this very afternoon vanishing altogether. In its place would be the still July heat, the rising chirp of iron bed legs moving on the wooden floor, the slipperiness of sweat on skin, the muffled cries. And afterwards, on the damp and empty sheets, the color of stains.

GOING HOME

WE NEEDED a smaller apartment, and soon. In three days my wife, Sandy, and I had to be out of this one-bedroom and into something cheaper. Things hadn't gone well for us in California. The jobs just weren't out here as we had heard. Every day we went out looking. We waited in lobbies with chrome and Naugahyde furniture and those broad-leafed rubber plants that seemed to thrive on fluorescent light and cigarette smoke. We filled out the applications, we underlined our phone number but no one ever called. No one, that is, except our parents back in Minnesota. They called every few days to see if we had found "anything," as they called it. They never said work. Anything. But maybe that was the right word. Sandy and I had been here six months and we were ready to take just about anything.

I drained my coffee cup, rinsed it, dried it, and put it in the cupboard. I spread out this morning's paper on the table. Sandy put yesterday's paper alongside. With a red pencil we went down the for-rent columns. We crossed them off, red *x*'s, one by one. We were looking for new listings, but there were none we did not recognize and most we had already called.

"What about this 'handyman special'?" Sandy asked. She drew a red arrow toward the number. "It's been listed for days. Maybe we should call."

I looked at the ad again:

Handyman special. One bdrm.
Fixup needed. U-work, U-save.
463–6000.

"Wonder what's wrong with it," I said.

"If we saw it, we'd know," she replied. She glanced at the kitchen clock, then at the calendar. "Maybe there's not much at all wrong with it," she said. "The sink, who knows? You can fix things like that."

"I don't have my tools," I answered. My tools were all back in Minnesota on my dad's farm. For some reason I had thought I wouldn't need any tools in California.

Sandy frowned and looked out the window. Sunlight bloomed in her blond hair and made it glow orange around the edges of her curls. Her skin was so clear, so white; I thought of how tanned everyone was here in California, everyone but her and me, who only sunburned pink.

"Let's call," I said. "We can take a look."

She dialed the number and waited. Someone must have answered, because she opened her lips and got ready to speak.

"But it's still available?" she repeated, nodding to me and pointing to the wall clock and smiling.

The man on the phone would meet us at the apartment in one half hour. Though the address was only a few minutes away, we left immediately. We were excited. Maybe things were changing for us.

The building was on the east edge of San Jose, next to the freeway, a white three-story affair with common balconies. Somebody's washing was spread along one of the railings. Below and across the street was an adult movie theater. Just down from the theater was a bus bench; four Mexican kids sat perched on it like crows on a fence. But Sandy and I didn't mind any of it. We waited in our Chevy and had fun trying to guess which of the oncoming cars belonged to the man on the phone. I guessed the red Triumph; Sandy guessed the new black

Turbo Saab; I tried a four-door Mercedes. But we should have known it was the bright blue Lincoln with the continental wheel on the trunk.

A man got out of the Lincoln and walked toward us. He had black hair and brown eyebrows. His face was very tan. A short leather jacket, the kind businessmen wear in California, was open over a blue-and-white Hawaiian-type shirt. The Hawaiian shirt was open several buttons, and a gold chain hung around his neck and down into the furry gray hair of his chest. The man could have been forty. He could have been sixty.

"Well, let's go on up and have a look," he said. He gave Sandy a long look, her breasts, her legs. She had on shorts, and I had her walk ahead of me up the stairs.

His apartment was on the far side of the building, so we had to walk down an inside hallway. After the bright sunlight the hallway was dim and brown. Passing other apartments, we could hear people speaking Spanish; could smell peppers and tomatoes frying. Some of the doors were open, but only the length of their safety chains.

The owner paused before the door and began to flip through a ring of similarly shaped keys. "Like the ad said," the man explained, as he slid the key into the lock, "the place needs a little work—Sheetrock and paint, mostly. My men would do it, but I'm a little short-handed these days. So I figure the new renter can do the work and save some money at the same time." He grinned at Sandy.

"Sounds good," Sandy murmured.

He smiled and swung open the door. At first it was difficult to see, because the inside drapes were drawn. I reached for the hall light, but only one of the four bulbs came on. Still, it didn't take much light to see the damage. The Sheetrock beside the door was broken, caved forward between the wall studs in a large diamond shape. It was as if somebody had taken a run and smashed himself into the wall. In the kitchen there were no light bulbs at all, but I could see brown smears across the white faces of the refrigerator and range. It was as if somebody had taken an old, torn paintbrush and had gone crazy

with brown paint. In the bedroom and living room there were
more smears, and more of those smashed diamonds of Sheetrock.

"Somebody had a real party, that's for sure," the man said.
His teeth glinted in the dim living room. He stood in front of
the cord that opened the drapes. I didn't like this.

"Maybe we could open the drapes," Sandy said. "It's hard to
see well without the light bulbs."

The man shrugged and stepped aside. Sandy pulled the cord
and daylight spilled into the room.

"Jesus," I said.

Sandy looked at me. She looked around again at the damage,
the smears, but she didn't see it. There were smears on the
walls, the carpet, even a spray of brown splotches on the ceiling. She didn't see it.

"That's blood," I said, keeping my voice calm, pointing to
the largest spray.

"Blood? Hey"—the man laughed—"get serious."

Sandy's mouth came open and she stepped closer to me.

"That's blood," I repeated. "I know blood when I see blood."
Sandy pulled me toward the door. I didn't resist.

"So what if it is," the man said. He grinned.

"Come on," Sandy whispered to me.

We walked away.

"Suit yourself, kids," the man called after us, "no sweat off
my ass. Somebody will take this apartment. Some people will
take anything."

"But not us!" I called back. "We won't take anything!" My
voice was shaking.

"Don't, please don't," Sandy whispered, pulling me into the
daylight toward our Chevy.

The engine caught on the first revolution and I pulled the
car into the traffic. I drove. We had nowhere to go but I kept
driving. It didn't matter. It seemed important to keep moving.
After a few miles of traffic lights Sandy started to cry and I
reached over and pulled her closer to me. By then we were
passing a city park that looked green and neat, so I stopped the

car. We got out and sat on a concrete bench. We sat there for a long while.

Across the park a man on a small John Deere tractor was pulling a long, spiked cylinder in even rows back and forth across the bright green grass. The cylinder's spikes flipped out little plugs of sod in a continuous shower. I knew what the man was doing: he was aerating the soil. In California, lawn grass grows so thickly it eventually chokes itself to death.

I picked up one of the sod plugs from in front of our bench. I crumbled it between my fingers. I held it briefly to my nose. It was September now in California, but the grass smelled like summertime in Minnesota and the black earth reminded me of my dad's farm. I watched the green tractor make its turn.

I spoke into Sandy's hair. "Maybe we ought to go back," I said.

She looked up at me.

"Back to the Midwest," I said.

WE TOOK only what we could pack into the Chevy. Our clothes. The books. The stereo. The plants. There was some furniture, but we left all that. Somebody else could use it. We didn't even wait for our damage deposit. I had enough money to get us at least into Nebraska, and Nebraska was in the Midwest, so I didn't worry about getting the rest of the way to Minnesota.

By four o'clock that afternoon we had left Oakland and Vacaville behind, and the Chevy pulled us into open country. Fields. Farms. Sandy and I began to talk. We told each other things we would do when we got back to the Midwest.

Sandy wanted to go canoeing at night on the Crow Wing River.

I wanted to help my father with some fall plowing, see my grandparents, split them some firewood.

We would look for work after that.

She and I talked on through Sacramento, all the way to the beginning foothills of the California Sierras, which seemed steeper than I had remembered them. We had a full car—the books were heavy—and as we climbed the steepening grade I began to watch the Chevy's oil and water temperature gauges. I had no reason to doubt the Chevy. I had always taken good care of it and it had never let me down. Yet both Sandy and I fell silent as we drove upward. Dusk fell. I turned on my headlights.

I began to think about the engine, about how the spark plugs and cylinders and camshaft and transmission and running gear all worked together; about how one small thing—a loose wire, a short, an oil seal—could break that whole rhythm that propelled us up these mountains. I began to hear engine noises. But the noise was only my own heartbeat drumming in my ears.

A light rain began to fall. We slowed through Gold Run and Blue Canyon. Westbound traffic heading into California was headlight-to-taillight, two lanes full, behind the blinking red lights of an accident. Eastbound traffic was lighter, but it, too, was slowing from the rain that was thickening to snow. I turned the wipers to a faster speed and slowed into second gear. We passed Emigrant Gap and headed toward the summit, Donner Pass. The Chevy's tires spun once on the watery snow. The snow thickened to wet, heavy leaves of white. Red taillights glowed. The wipers slapped harder and harder to keep up. My shirt was damp, the steering wheel slick in my hands.

Suddenly we topped Donner Pass. I felt the Chevy lighten and start to run freely. I shifted back into third gear and took my foot off the gas; we could nearly coast now. The snowflakes lightened some. I wiped my hands and looked across to Sandy.

"Some music?" she said. She smiled.

"Sure," I said. I had forgotten about the radio. We hadn't listened to it the whole trip.

Sandy clicked on the radio to static. She rolled the dial, but couldn't pick up any stations because of the snow.

"Sorry."

"It's all right by me," I said.

She turned to look out her side window, into the night.

I reached out my arm and pulled her closer. She leaned in

to me, and stared at the snow. In another mile or so she was asleep on my shoulder.

The snow began to let up. With each pass of the wipers I could see farther into the darkness ahead. I drove and stared through the windshield and thought about Sandy. About us, together. Our lives.

As I drove down the mountain I began to see through the night into our lives to come. I saw Sandy and me at Christmas with our parents, all of us circled around the tree, its colored lights twinkling in our eyes. I saw Sandy and me ahead some years, saw children running toward us wanting to be caught and swung into the air, then caught again. I even saw Sandy and me gray and old, and that wasn't bad, either.

I turned to her. I wanted to wake her and tell her these things, but they wouldn't have made much sense, and anyway, she needed the sleep. Instead, I just kept driving, as the weather lifted, straight ahead into that clearing, blue night.

THE TRAPPER

SOMEONE HAD sneaked up on Feller. Crouched in the ditch, bent over the mouth of the culvert, his hands in its cold gurgle of water, Feller felt eyes.

He whirled and saw shoes. On the roadbed above him were shoes with turned-up toes and zigzag tread. (That track, he had seen that running track this summer on the road past his cabin.) From the shoes rose short, muscular legs thick-furred with brown hair. The legs ended in red shorts. Above the shorts was a blue T-shirt with a broad tongue of sweat up its center. The bound ends of two brown braids of hair jerked Fuller's eyes up to a woman's face.

She was the ugliest woman Feller had ever seen. Her face was wide and flat, punctured in its middle by small, pinched-together blue eyes—a shovel held up to the sky with two .22 slugs shot through its center. Though he had never before seen this woman, it was clear to Feller that she was the reason he had never married.

"What is it you're doing?" the woman asked.

Feller's eyes flickered to his basket of traps on the bank. Her eyes followed his.

"Setting a trap," Feller said. From disuse his voice croaked like a magpie. Living alone in the woods, Feller did not have to talk to many people. He liked it that way.

"Setting a trap for what?"

Feller stared. "Mink," he answered. His heart began to thud in his chest as if he, not she, had been running. For there was nothing wrong with trapping mink. It was September in northern Minnesota and trapping season had just opened. Feller had his license in his left shirt pocket. At age seventy-two, he had been trapping in these creeks for fifty years.

"Why set a trap for a mink? A mink never set a trap for you," the woman said.

Feller stood up. The woman was very short, but on the road she towered above him. He could smell her sweat, a sharp odor like fox spray. He stared at her and felt dry air in his mouth.

Why he trapped. The question made no sense. He had always trapped. He made his sets at the mouths of culverts, among the wet rocks in the streams. The mink he carried home swayed heavy in his jacket pockets. In his cabin he skinned them, then stretched their fur on flat pine paddles and hung them on his storeroom wall to dry. Later in the winter he took the thirty or more pelts to Duluth where he sold the brown fur for green cash. The money, along with his social security check, allowed Feller to remain in his cabin another summer. Without the mink money Feller would have to go on welfare. Then a man in a suit, a man driving a government car, would come for Feller. He would haul Feller to the city. There the welfare man would put Feller in a white-walled apartment no bigger than a bear's den. Feller would have to cook on a stove that raised no flame, drink water that tasted like piss, and listen to people who lived only a pine stud away, four inches through the wall.

Feller would not last long in an apartment. Then the welfare man would come for him again. He would lock Feller in a rest home where all things smelled of piss, where white-haired people lay on the floor with their hands jammed into their crotches and moaned for someone to put a slug through their brainpans.

No town for Feller.

He set his jaw. "Some people trap, some don't," he said.

"I don't trap," she said. "No one should set traps for anything. Imagine you were walking along a river when suddenly
some kind of iron clamp leaped up and crushed your legs and
held you there until someone came along and clubbed you
over the head and then peeled off your hide and sent it to
New York City where it was made into coats for rich women
to wear, how would *you* like that?"

Feller's basket of traps lay on the bank halfway to the
woman. Without taking his eyes from hers he slowly leaned
down, then jerked them to safety. He made his way up the
bank to his pickup.

She followed him. "We should protect and love all the animals," she said. "If everybody kills the animals, then in two
or three years there won't be any animals. And it's the animals, like dolphins and whales and who knows, even mink,
who can talk to us through nature if only we listened. We've
got to start listening to the animals because it's only the animals who can save us from ruining this world, but most people can't see that."

Inside his truck, his hand out of sight below the door, Feller
eased forward the lock. The ignition key trembled briefly over
its slot, then fit. The engine caught on the first turn.

She jogged alongside as he let out the clutch. She called to
him, "We have to live for the animals. That's why I moved
up here—somebody has to live for the animals!"

Feller spun the tires. The woman began to shrink in his
mirror. The road curved, and just before she swung sideways
from sight, Feller saw her stop running. He saw her look back
toward the creek.

FELLER AWOKE very early the next morning; his east windows
were still black. He awoke with the ugly woman squarely in
the center of his head as if she were framed in the doorway
of his cabin. In his dream the woman had been running through
the woods chased by her own face.

He went to the water pail and splashed cold water into his

eyes. Then he cooked breakfast, two eggs and strip of salt pork. The woman's face came back in the black frying pan.

Moved here. Feller looked up from the stove. She had said moved here. Feller swore. He did not mind the occasional campers with their canoes and little Eskimo-type boats who came on Friday afternoon and always left on Sunday, but now in the woods there were more and more smoke-puffing A-frames and larger, barn-faced cabins with window glass across the whole front. This summer he had heard the coyote whine of a power saw, and once, the sound of one hammer, nailing. Her. That had been the ugly woman. Moved here to live for the animals. Feller swallowed the egg yolks, left his plate on the table, and hurriedly laced his boots.

Pink light in the poplar tops, blue light among the trunks, Feller slid down the bank where the woman had surprised him. His trap held a stick. A dead branch stood upright in its jaws like a withered Christmas tree in a tin clamp. On the sand beside the water was the zigzag print of the woman's shoes. Feller pitched the trap and its stick up onto the road.

He drove on to the next culvert. Her running tracks, fresh in the soft center dirt, led him down the road. His heart began to thud. He sped up. Near the creek the woman's long strides shortened, slowed to a walk. At the culvert her footprints disappeared over the bank. Without leaving his truck Feller saw the stick in his trap. He slid down the bank. Beside the woman's tracks were the smaller, crabbed prints of a big buck mink who had detoured around Feller's sprung iron. Feller cursed. His voice echoed down the river.

He drove on. Chokecherry Creek was sandy and rockless, too open for a good set, so Feller had placed his trap a ways downstream alongside a fallen, water-melted pine, the kind where crayfish liked to hide. A big buck mink, spitting, walnut-colored, shrank back the length of the trap's wire and bared its teeth. Feller unstrapped his hatchet. Afterwards, when the mink was heavy in his jacket pouch, Feller stood and squinted upstream. He measured, with his eyes, the distance from his trap to the road.

BACK IN his cabin, Feller lit a fire in the wood stove. The rest
of his traps had held only sticks. That bitch of a woman. Still
in his jacket, Feller leaned close to the heat and thought.

He could not catch mink with sticks in his traps.

He could not catch mink in the back of his pickup where
all his traps now lay in a jumble of wire.

He tried to think of what he must do, but the woman's
shovel face, her hairy man's legs filled his mind. He sat up,
took out his pocketknife and began to skin the mink while it
was still warm.

Mink were smart animals.

The man from welfare was smarter than mink.

But so far Feller had outsmarted them both.

The ugly woman might be strong, but she was certainly
not smart. Not with a face like hers. So Feller would have to
outsmart her, too. Drawing the pelt inside out, peeling it
slowly down the slippery carcass, working his fingers along
the body as though removing a tight sock from a foot, Feller
pulled away the hide; at the head, which came last, he cut
carefully around the eyes, the lips, and lastly the nose. With
a final tug, the carcass fell away. Feller ran his arm inside the
skin. The fur was cool on his bare arm. With the edge of
the knife blade Feller slowly scraped fat and thought about the
ugly woman. Sometime later he looked up and smiled. Immediately he felt sleepy. He hung the pelt on the iron rail of
his cot and, fully dressed, fell into his bed.

Sunlight.

Feller awoke from his nap with yellow light full in his
windows. He rose, ate a small chunk of smoked venison, drank
down a cup of applesauce, then went to his storeroom to find
his rubber hipboots.

In the cold room on the board walls hung his traps. Feller ran
his hand over their iron as he passed. Number 0's were for
gophers and weasels, their mouths no bigger than a woman's
fist. Number 1's, the size of a saucer, were for his mink. Number 2 double springs, the size of pie tins, were for fox. Number 3's, slightly bigger, were for coyotes. Number 4's, dou-

bled-springed with teeth, were for timber wolves. At the end of the storeroom hung his number 8 bear trap. Its irons were as long as Feller's leg; when set, its mouth was as big as a washtub. Feller ran his hand down its cold iron. His fingers came away smudged red with rust.

At Chokecherry Creek, clumsy in his hipboots, Feller clambered down the bank. Before the ugly woman he had never needed more than overshoes. Now, along with the hipboots and his basket of traps, he carried his kitchen broom. He stepped into the deeper water and headed downstream. A cold thorn of stream water was leaking inside his right boot at the ankle. He kept walking.

Feller began to see mink droppings, furry black seeds on the rocks. But he continued downstream. Where the river bent east and hid the road from sight, Feller slowed. He set his traps in the shallow water among the rocks. He twisted their wires around the small alders at the water's edge. Then he headed back upstream. At the culvert he unstrapped the broom. He swept water over his boot tracks on the sand until his prints melted away. On the road he dusted gravel over the rest of his tracks, then drove on.

Returning to his cabin that evening, Feller had to use the headlights of his truck. Inside, he undressed. From the extra walking in heavy boots his shirt was wet through with sweat. His right foot, from the leaking stream water, felt gone. He tugged off the boot and lit a fire in the stove. He lay on his cot and propped the cold leg on a chair close to the heat. Sometime later he awoke to the smell of burning hair—he jerked away his leg. As he chafed the heat from his flesh, the singed hair rubbed away until the skin of his calf was smooth and red and hairless.

SOMEONE. Feller jerked awake. There was noon light outside the cabin. Boards creaked again on his front porch. Someone was out there.

Feller's heart began a quicker pumping that thudded in his

ears. He stared at the unlocked door. His shotgun was in the storeroom across the loud plain of old floorboards.

Someone knocked. Sharp, solid raps, five of them. Feller eased from his cot and crept along the wall where the boards did not squeak. He closed his hand over the doorknob.

"Mr. Feller? Mr. Alvin Feller?" a voice called.

Her. The woman. Feller tightened his grip on the knob.

She knocked again, then tried to open the door. Feller used both hands to keep the knob from turning; he could feel her through the iron. Finally she released her grip. Feller's heart bounced inside his chest.

"Mr. Feller, I know you're in there because your pickup is outside and your hipboots are here drying on the porch. If you don't want to come out that's okay, but I found some things that belong to you. I'll leave them out here."

There were several thuds and the clank of steel. The porch boards creaked, then were silent. Feller waited a long time. Finally he eased to the side of the window and looked out. Far down his driveway the woman, dressed in red, bobbed evenly away toward the main road. On the porch in a jumble of wire and chain lay all Feller's traps.

And something else.

A small loaf of bread.

Feller circled the bread, then bent down for a closer look. A small loaf of dark bread. Feller found a stick. He speared the loaf, and with a curse, flung it far out into the woods.

THE NEXT WEEK, and all of October, Feller carried his traps farther downstream. He walked in the water until the tag alders and red willows choked the riverbank and the creek tunneled beneath their overhang. He set his traps beside the slippery, heavy trees that lay in the water, beside boulders that rose up big as cars. On the way back upstream Feller made sure to leave five or six traps in the clearer sand eddies. There the black pans of the traps stood out like round, open eyes on the face of the stream.

Evenings Feller sat in his chair facing the cabin door. With the lights out, he drank tea and waited. Sometime near sundown his porch boards creaked and his traps began to thud onto the boards. He counted them with his fingers—three, four, five . . . six. When the thudding stopped and the boards creaked again, Feller waited, then went to the window to watch the woman jogging away. Outside on his porch he looked for her gift. Sometimes it was bread, sometimes a piece of pie, sometimes cookies. Each night Feller took a shovel, lifted the food, carried it to the edge of the yard and slung it into the woods.

By Halloween, Feller had fourteen pelts stretched and drying on their paddles. And there would have been more. On account of the extra walking, the thicker brush, and the larger stones downstream, Feller could check his most distant sets only every third day. Twice the coyotes had winded his catch and left him only mink claws in the jaws of the traps. Bastards. But if Feller had not completely fooled the coyotes at least he had outsmarted the ugly woman.

The next evening Feller made his pot of tea and sat down to wait. He sipped from his cup. With his pocketknife he peeled shavings from a soft pine limb. He hummed a little tune. By nine o'clock the teapot was empty. He checked his watch again. The woman was usually on time. He swept the shavings into the stove and watched them flare red. He made more tea. After an hour, his heart, like a faraway telegraph, began to tap out a faint message in his chest. Feller waited as the words came one by one into his head.

The ugly woman was gone.

He was free.

Free!

Feller rummaged in his cabinet for the whiskey bottle. He blew dust from the cap, then poured himself half a cup. But Feller had taken only one sip when something crashed against his door. The whiskey trembled in his cup.

He counted.

Five . . . six . . . seven.

Eleven . . . twelve . . . sixteen.

Further.

Twenty-three . . . twenty-four.

Then the porch was silent.

Feller trembled all over. He did not trust himself to stand. Finally he forced himself upright from the chair. He eased open the cabin door. There on the porch lay every one of his traps.

And no gift.

FELLER WORKED harder. He set thirty traps, forty. No time for his cabin, he carried his lunch of bread, cold venison, and an apple in his heavy basket of traps. Often he forgot to eat. When he remembered, he paused along the stream, gulped down the food, then lay back to rest. The ground now in early November was cold enough to keep him from sleeping more than a few minutes. But soon he dared not close his eyes.

Once, lying in the tall grass along Leaf Creek, Feller started awake. Just across and upstream, moving his way through the poplars, came something red. The woman. Feller shrank deeper into the grass. He watched. Her broad, flat face drew light from the stream as every few feet she leaned over the bank to look into the water. Then she looked carefully at the base of the small trees along the bank.

Wires. That's how she found the traps. The bank wires.

She came closer, directly across the stream. Feller could have cast a light fly and hooked her. Her braids hung forward and her small eyes moved from rock to rock. Feller did not move or even blink. In the grass he was a rabbit and she the wolf; she would hear his heartbeat.

But intent on the stream, the ugly woman passed without looking up. Feller swallowed. He lay back and stared into the sky until his heartbeat slowed. She had outsmarted him. He needed another plan.

IN THE storeroom of his cabin Feller rummaged through his gear until he found the plow irons. Forearm-long, as flat as cleavers, as cold and heavy as stream stone, the irons had once been used as drags when Feller had trapped coyotes in open, treeless country. The plow irons would work as well in water.

The next day Feller teetered downstream beneath the added weight of the irons. The straps of the basket cut into his shoulders like snare wires. His shoulder blades grated against each other.

Rest. Walk. Rest again. Finally Feller reached a bend in the river where the trees shut out the daylight. There he set his traps among the big rocks. He wired each chain to a plow iron, then buried the iron in the streambed. She was not so smart. Not with a face like hers.

Once, while his hands were in the cold water, two stones rolled together on Feller's fingers. Blood drifted like smoke from beneath his fingernails. He moaned, and held the pinched hand submerged until it was numb.

The weight of the plow irons and the extra walking cut Feller's work down to only two creeks. But the next day his traps held two buck mink and a small female. His cabin smelled again of fresh mink fat. That night he sat soaking his swollen fingers in a saucer of whiskey. He faced the door, waiting. Once outside a fox barked. The wood rustled inside the stove. He waited late but there was no sudden squeak on the porch, no crash of traps. At midnight Feller dried his fingers and drank down the saucer of whiskey.

THE FOLLOWING day Feller's traps held two more mink. He added more irons to his pack, another creek to his legs. He still had only nineteen mink.

In the next days Feller ate when he remembered to, then only coffee and a bowl of applesauce. His skinning kept him up past midnight. In the morning he left the cabin by starlight. Once on his porch he saw reflected in a windowpane a wild, white-haired, gaunt stranger. Feller whirled but there was no one there. He laughed, and his voice croaked back from the trees.

Two DAYS later, near midnight, a crash on Feller's porch drove his skinning knife deep into his thumb. He listened, frozen. One by one his traps and their irons clanged against the cabin wall like the tolling of some great clock.

Feller did not go to bed that night. He stayed close to the stove. The cabin felt cold. The weather was changing. It was mid-November now. And only twenty mink. And no traps in the water. Twice in the night he went to the storeroom to count them again.

He remained inside the cabin all the next day except to carry in armloads of wood. He kept the fire blazing but he could not get warm. In the afternoon he put on his jacket and went again to the storeroom. Twenty. The mink hung flat and inside out on their paddles. He stared at them. His heart began to drum in his ears as if he had been working hard. Or running.

Running. That was it. He had been running. From the ugly woman. For two months he been running. She was the trapper, not Feller. Now she had him cornered.

Feller touched one of the mink pelts. There were hard veins of fat on the flesh side, cool fur underneath. He thought of the mink in his traps. How they tore at the iron with their mouths. How they chewed at the wire and broke away their teeth. That failing, how they gnawed through their own legs. How at the end, when Feller approached, they snarled and spit even at the falling swing of the hatchet.

He turned to stare at his wall of traps. Heart roaring in his ears, Feller reached for the bear trap.

AT DAWN Feller was a mile down Leaf Creek. On his back he carried the bear trap, a shovel, and a burlap sack. He followed the same trail on which he had seen the ugly woman. Here and there in the faint animal path he saw her zigzag track. Every thirty steps he stopped to lean the trap against a tree and catch his breath.

Two miles downstream he reached the bend where she had almost caught him. He stopped to stare at the narrow trail. Beside a rotted poplar that lay across the path Feller struggled

free of the bear trap. When he stopped panting, he spread the
burlap bag alongside the trail. With the shovel's point he stabbed
through the thin frozen crust of dirt until the earth softened.
Then he began to shovel the dirt onto the burlap. The dirt
smelled of rotted leaves and roots and angleworms.

Twenty minutes later Feller lifted the bear trap into the
hole. From his belt he unhooked two screw clamps. He fitted
them on the trap springs and slowly turned their cranks. The
springs creaked open. The jaws of the trap slackened, then
fell open. The bear trap fit the hole like false teeth in a mouth.

Now for the trigger. Feller eased his fingers beneath the
hand-sized pan and felt for the trigger. Steady. When the trigger was engaged, Feller carefully loosened first one clamp,
then the other. Steady. Slow. The pan of the trap quivered
but held. Finally the clamps were free and Feller jerked away
his hands. He sat back to catch his breath. The trap grinned
up from the dirt. Its pan was a black throat into the earth.

Feller leaned away and stood up. He sprinkled fresh dirt
inside the trap and over the springs. Next he chafed dead grass
over the black dirt. He carried armfuls of leaves and winnowed
them over the grass. The leftover dirt he carried and threw
into the river, where he watched it dissolve away in the water like smoke in the wind. Finally he stepped backwards on
the trail and surveyed the set from all angles.

There was no trap. There were only dead leaves on a narrow trail.

THAT EVENING Feller fried himself a big supper of potatoes
and venison. He cut the meat into small, even squares. He
made himself chew slowly. His plate was streaked gray with
grease before he remembered the potatoes, still on the stove.
He was not hungry but he ate them anyway.

At sundown he poured a cup of whiskey and turned his
chair to face the door.

Near midnight a horned owl hooted. A second owl answered
from farther west. He put two more sticks of wood on the
fire. Catching ablaze, the dry wood rustled like burning leaves.

Feller sat in his chair sipping whiskey until the black light in his windows turned blue. Then gray. Then pink. He went to bed at dawn and slept all day.

At sundown Feller awoke, fried venison and made tea. After supper he poured whiskey. Near midnight the two owls hooted again. Much later a fox barked. Feller sipped from his cup until his east window pinkened to yellow. Then, stiffly, he rose and slowly opened the cabin door. He walked onto the porch. He pissed over the railing. On a pine tree a gray nuthatch pecked at a worm hole. Two chickadees chirped on the choke-berry bush. Feller sat on his porch in the raw sunlight. For a long time he listened to the birds and the squirrels, their peck and chatter. He had forgotten that the birds and animals talked so much. That there were so many of them.

FOR THE NEXT several days Feller slept. He rose only to eat and piss, then fell back into bed. Daylight came and went in his windows. He kept track of the days but did not bother with the time. He had not slept so well in weeks. Maybe months. Once he awoke to a different daylight in the cabin. He looked outside to see two inches of fresh, wet snow. Everything was white and clean and new.

BY THE MIDDLE of December Feller felt rested enough to re-main out of bed during the day. He sheared away the white hair that hung in his eyes. He clipped and sanded his finger-nails. He worked with a knife on his toenails, which, like the teeth of sick beaver, had begun to curve back into his flesh.

Finished with himself, he turned to the cabin. He swept and scoured the board floor. He scraped away spoonfuls of black grease from the stove top. He washed dishes and put them away. When his cabin was in order, Feller returned to his storeroom.

On the wall hung the faint outline of the bear trap. The trap was gone. He did not let himself remember where. Traps got lost. Traps came and went. Trouble. There had been some trouble with his traps this fall. That's why he had only twenty mink so far. But there was still open water. And good trailing snow, too. He could still make thirty. The trouble was over now.

That night Feller stayed up late boiling and dyeing his mink traps. He hummed a little tune as he checked their springs and wires. He held his overshoes up to the fire's light to look for holes, then laid out his clothes and boots for tomorrow.

In bed Feller tried to think of what had been the trouble this season. Bad luck. That was all that he could think of. But that was over now. Feller smiled. He closed his eyes and felt his cot begin its slow turning.

MUCH LATER that night a tremendous crash threw Feller from his bed. The noise threw him across the cabin and up against his door as if he were nailed to its wood. His heart shuddered out of control.

Outside there was a shuffling sound. Then silence. Feller waited, panting for air. Finally he forced himself to the side of the window. He looked out.

On the porch, glinting in the moonlight, lay his bear trap. Beyond in the yard was a dark figure moving across the snow. It was the woman. She was moving steadily down the driveway, not running this time, for between her crutches was one dark leg and a long white cast on the other. But even on crutches she was taking enormous strides.

Feller jerked back from the window. In a rush his breath went out of him. Try and try as he might, he could not catch it again.

BLOOD PRESSURE

My husband, Harold, is an early morning walker and he was first to notice, just beyond our driveway, the swerving tracks across the ditch, the broken barbed wire, the channel of flattened corn disappearing into the field.

He came into the house panting. "Some blue car—the driver, he's—"

"Easy," I told him. Harold's face had gone redder than the sun just coming up, his cheeks scarlet below his white hair. I made him sit down while I called the sheriff. After Harold had caught his wind I drove him back to the field.

In the ditch the tracks were black scars across green grass. We got out of the car and crossed the ditch, passing the curls of barbed wire, the beady bright eyes of their broken ends, and went into the field. We walked quickly but the June corn was flat and tangled beneath our feet and made for hard going. We couldn't run. We're both seventy. We had ourselves to think of. Soon enough, fifty yards into the field, I saw it, a long blue car draped with corn leaves. Its roofline lay even with the tops of the corn. The car looked like one robin's egg in a great green nest.

A long blue car. An older Cadillac. "Doc Langenson—" Harold and I said at the same moment.

On the highway a siren began to wail. Harold and I looked

behind, at the road, then at each other, then at the Cadillac. We stepped closer.

In the front seat I could see someone slumped against the steering wheel. I saw white hair. My heart began to thud in my ears. I could feel my blood pressure rising.

"Martha?" Harold said.

"I'm all right," I answered.

We came alongside the car. I didn't know what to expect. Harold and I bent to look inside. It was Doc, all right, but his face was so dark. "Blood pools and settles and darkens the skin at death." I'd read that somewhere, or maybe saw it on TV, some detective show. But then I saw his face—his chin and cheeks and forehead and ears, the lips, even the open eyes— all of it was bearded with mosquitos. I sat down hard in the cornstalks.

LATER that morning people from town came out to look at the accident site. Our farm sits just beyond the city limits of Springfield, Iowa, the first place heading out of town or the last one heading in, depending which way you're going. People parked in our driveway, along the field, in the ditches. Harold and I stayed by the road and directed parking. We answered any questions we could. We felt in some way responsible; after all, it had happened on our land.

By mid-morning everyone from town seemed to be in the field, so Harold and I joined them around Doc's car. The coroner had long ago taken Doc to town, but people still leaned down and shaded their eyes to see inside the Cadillac.

"Attention everybody!" someone called from behind.

We all turned. Velma Hansen—I could tell her by her short hair, the blue pincurls—stood with a black camera, one of those new narrow ones, sideways across her eyes. For a moment I thought of the raccoons that come into the field at night, how they climb up the stalks, break them over, trying to get at the corn when the ears are in milk.

"Stand a little closer together," she called.

We looked at each other, then stepped closer together. When

someone has a camera it's funny how you do what they say.

"Hold it . . ." she said. She made some adjustment to the camera. We waited. Mosquitos whined in the cool, damp dirt around the cornstalks and lit on my ankles. We didn't dare move. Finally the camera clicked.

"Hold steady—just one more to make sure!" she called.

AFTER the photos, the sheriff asked us to stand back while he did some measuring. He hooked the bent finger end of a steel tape to the driver's door, then walked backwards toward the road, toward daylight. The tape unwound. It stretched, drooping in the sunlight, like a power line between its poles. At the fence the sheriff called out, "Sixty yards!"

"Man, he must have been traveling," someone said.

"Never any question about that," the sheriff said.

We looked to the sheriff and there was a chuckle or two. In Springfield, Doc Langenson had his own traffic laws. His Cadillac sailed down the highway, skidded around corners, bounded up long driveways, swooped into yards. In emergencies he took shortcuts through picket fences, across lawns, over begonia beds and cedar shrubs. On the open road his Cadillac arrowed past farm pickups and cars like a bluebird swooping through a flock of barnyard sparrows. The Doc seldom drove under ninety no matter whether he carried in his back seat a farmer with a tractor-crushed leg or only his set of golf clubs. The sheriff, the city policeman, and certainly the rest of us didn't care how Doc Langenson drove. He was our doctor. We were glad to have him.

Which brought something to mind.

I must have spoken aloud because everyone turned to look at me.

Harold slowly shook his head. "Martha, you've got no appointment on Friday because Springfield's got no doctor."

WE ALL MET at the café the next afternoon. Main Street is one block of red brick buildings with a new yellow Quik-Stop gas station at one end and the school at the other. The café is centered on Main Street. Fred Lynde from the hardware store began things, as always.

"You lose your doctor, you lose your clinic," Fred said. "And you lose your clinic, you lose the young families. You lose the kids, you lose your school. You lose the school, you lose Main Street," he said. Fred always talked in rows of words that made me see the inside of his store. The straight racks of hardware. The narrow aisles. The square corners.

When Fred finished, no one said anything; what he described had already happened to nearby Kensville and Holdingtown, too. Both towns now were just truck stops along the highway.

Then someone said, "So we got to get another doctor."

"And fast," somebody added.

"How?"

"Advertise," John Harper answered. He published the town newspaper, *The Springfield Independent*.

"But not locally," Ken Anderson said immediately. Ken's and John's boys were the same age and shared quarterback duties on the football team.

"So where, then?" John Harper said.

Ken shrugged. He thought a moment. "Maybe . . . a larger city. Like Des Moines. Some place where there's a doctor looking to get away from the rat race."

"That's right," Velma Hansen said. She was the reporter for the newspaper, and did oil paintings from her photographs; she was also president of the Springfield Arts Council, a group of four of us. "Springfield might be a small town but it's got a lot to offer," she said.

We were silent.

We all looked at each other.

"Well, let's get on with it, then," Fred said.

We began work on the advertisement. I did the writing—that is, I wrote down what everyone finally agreed upon:

> Springfield, Iowa, pop. 426,
> needs family-type physician.
> Quiet town. Clean air

and water. No crime, drugs or
racial tension. Only 100 miles
to Des Moines.

The ad ran for one week in the *Des Moines Register*, the
Cedar Rapids Gazette, and *The Iowa City Iowan*.

There was no response. No letters.

The next week we tried the *Minneapolis Tribune*, *Fargo
Forum*, and the *Wisconsin State Journal* in Madison.

Nothing. Two weeks of nothing.

We met again in the café. "Maybe it's written wrong," Fred
Lynde said. "Maybe it should read all in one sentence, with
commas or something." He ran his hand through his hair, that
is, where it used to be. I remembered his hair, coppery, then
pale yellow, then white, then gone. Women remember more
things than men. Men's minds drive straight ahead like a
fast train heading down the tracks, but along the way things
keep loosening, slipping off, disappearing. Women's minds are
longer, heavier, more tightly packed because they don't lose
or just plain give up on what's past.

"We're doing something wrong," Fred murmured.

I spoke up. "Doctors in Cedar Rapids and Iowa City and
Des Moines and Minneapolis live there because they want to,"
I said. "Because they like it. They can always drive to the
country on the weekend. Maybe we should advertise in some
very large cities far away from here. On the East or the West
Coast, for example. To a doctor living there, Springfield might
sound like a dream come true."

Everyone turned to stare at me. I felt my ears warm.

"Martha's right," Ken Anderson said.

"I read where more doctors live in Washington, D.C., than
anywhere in the world," I added.

"There you go," Fred Lynde said. "Listen to the woman."

I felt my neck warm. Fred and I used to smile at each other
when no one else was looking. But that was forty years ago.

We ran the ad in the Sunday *Washington Post*. Two more
weeks of nothing.

Then, a letter. Just one letter, but we didn't stop to think about that. "G. T. Sonnenfeld, M.D.," the return address read. Fred tore it open. We waited while his eyes scanned down the page.

"Yes!" Fred said.

We clapped, then passed the letter around.

The doctor was without doubt interested. He wrote that he'd like to try out Springfield for one year, see how it went. His signature was a brief scrawl across the bottom of the page.

"He's a real doctor," Fred Lynde said, holding up the letter, pointing to the signature.

We smiled at that. Then the letter passed hand to hand around the café again. We nodded. The one-year tryout, the one-year trial part didn't bother us. We knew once we got the doctor and his wife here—once they saw everything Springfield had to offer—they'd stay. Of that we were sure. When we left the café on Main Street, the sunlight shone coppery on the bricks, and glass glinted bright in the post office and on the other store windows. Main Street was smiling.

OVER THE next two weeks Harold and I exchanged several letters with the Sonnenfelds. Most of their letters were from Trudy Sonnenfeld, brief notes in handwriting not unlike her husband's. Trudy Sonnenfeld appeared to handle all the arrangements in the family. The dates. The move itself. She even asked detailed questions about the clinic and its staff. But that was only right, for we knew how busy doctors were.

She mentioned, too, that her husband had always wanted to live in the country, even have some cattle.

Harold and I wrote that there was a small farmstead, the old Whittier place, for rent. It was close to town, actually just down the road from our own farm. We said we'd be happy to help them get started with the cattle, show them the ropes.

She wrote back and said the Whittier place sounded just fine. She enclosed a deposit.

The day before the doctor was to arrive we strung up a

welcoming banner in town, two king-sized white sheets with red lettering. WELCOME DR. & MRS. SONNENFELD. It fluttered across Main Street. A group of us waited at the café, sitting where we could watch the street. We waited most of the next day, and tried to guess which car might be theirs, but at suppertime had to go home. Late in the night I woke up to noise over at the Whittier place in the night. The yard light was on. I heard a car door slam.

"They're here!" I said to Harold. But he lay still and breathed evenly.

"They're here," I said, softer, to myself.

THE NEXT morning, at exactly eight o'clock, Dr. Gertrude "Trudy" Sonnenfeld strode into the Springfield Community Clinic.

A woman doctor!

In Springfield!

The news ran up and down Main Street.

Two retired men with prostate trouble said they'd drive to Des Moines from now on. The rest of us tried to think it through. A woman doctor in our town seemed modern. That was the word which kept coming up. Modern. Modern times. The modern world. Though we never talked about it, we all knew Springfield hadn't kept up. There were fewer children nowadays. The graduating class was down to eighteen; they left Springfield to find jobs in Des Moines or Minneapolis, and came back only on holidays. Secretly we all knew Springfield was in trouble, but a woman doctor . . . By ten o'clock that morning we believed that Dr. Sonnenfeld and her husband were just what this town needed.

I WAS ONE of her first patients. Just a blood pressure check. I have some trouble with that. I waited in the little examining room. I could hear my heartbeat slowly speeding up. My blood pressure always rises when I wait for the doctor, so I try to occupy my mind. I looked one by one at the things on the counter and in the stainless steel tray. A stethoscope. Rubber gloves. Cotton swabs that reminded me of popped corn in a glass jar. A tube of that clear jelly. Some brown rubber tubing. Some plastic syringes.

I leaned over and lifted one of the syringes. It was surprisingly light; I wondered what a syringe felt like full.

I touched the tube of jelly. Its metal skin was cool and I drew back my fingers. "Water soluble, non-staining personal lubricant." It occurred to me that in a big city like Washington, D.C., a doctor could not leave these things lying out in the open. People would steal them. People would steal things and sell them. Or people would use what they'd stolen on themselves. The syringes. The jelly.

Just then the door swung open. I sat up straight.

Dr. Sonnenfeld was a tall, strong woman with broad shoulders. She had a square, wide face and round blue eyes and brown bangs cut straight across her forehead an inch lower than was becoming. She reminded me of some of the women who drive tractors for their husbands.

"Martha? Granlund?" she said, glancing down at my chart.

I smiled and nodded.

"I'm Trudy Sonnenfeld." She held out her hand and smiled briefly.

I shook her hand. It was strong and wide like the rest of her. "Dr. Sonnenfeld," I said.

"Call me Trudy," she said, rolling up my sleeve.

My ears warmed. "All right," I said. "Trudy."

She looped the blood pressure band around my arm and pulled tight its hook and pile, pulled it a lot tighter than Doc Langenson ever had. She pumped the black ball. She began to speak when we heard a loud voice in the waiting room—a high-pitched man's voice. She kept pumping the bulb, but slower, as she listened.

"Damn," she said.

Suddenly the door jolted open and a man stood in the doorway. Then he came right over to us.

I caught my breath; what if I'd been undressed?

"Why didn't you wake me?" the man said to Trudy Sonnenfeld. His voice was small and anxious. He was a tiny, narrow-shouldered man with a pale face and a curly mop of dark hair. For a moment I thought he was a teenager, but the creases around his eyes and mouth said he was well into his forties. I thought of that disease where young children age too fast and look like old men and women when they're only teenagers or younger even than that.

"I woke up in this house and I didn't know where I was," the man said. "Why didn't you wake me?"

Trudy Sonnenfeld raised her hand to put it on his shoulder. He flinched. "You've interrupted my work and you've startled one of my patients," she said.

He squinted at her, his face still turned slightly to the side.

"I want you to get a grip on yourself," she continued.

He tried to look away but she turned his narrow face to hers. "I want you to go back to the house," she said. Her voice fell to a flat monotone. "I want you to start unpacking the car. Start with the books. Then work on the dishes. And buy some groceries on the way home."

The man squinted up at her. "I don't know any stores," he said.

My arm tingled; she still held shut the little rubber ball. "There's Don's Mart at the south end of town," I said. "You can't miss it."

The doctor looked briefly at me, then back at her husband. "There you go," she said to him.

"I believe thick-cut pork chops are on special."

The doctor and her husband looked at each other, then at me.

The doctor's husband giggled, a sharp, rapid laugh.

"We're not big meat-eaters," Dr. Sonnenfeld said to me.

"Oh," I said, but the word came out in a small grunt of pain. The doctor bent to my arm. Its veins bulged like roots, roots coming out of the ground after a heavy rain, gray ground, dark roots.

"Thick-cut chops," her husband said from behind her, his small, shiny eyes on his wife. "Shall I buy us some thick-cut chops?"

"I want you out of here," the doctor said between her teeth, watching the clock and counting with her lips as the air hissed away. "When I look up I want you gone."

"Okay, okay," he said, backing away from us. He went out the door.

With a quick jerk Dr. Sonnenfeld tore loose the arm band. Briefly she chafed my flesh. "I'm sorry," she said. She turned away and hung up the strap. "That was my husband, Winston."

I flexed my wrist, my hand. For a moment I couldn't feel my fingers. Then they began a prickling return. "He seems . . . like a nice man," I murmured.

She turned away to write on my chart. "In many ways he's just a child," she said.

WHEN I GOT home, Harold looked up from his newspaper. "So how did it go at the clinic?" he asked. He smiled at me with his round face, his wide eyes.

"All right, I guess," I said. I went to the window and pretended to look out.

"Just all right?" he asked.

"I met them both," I said. "Her and her husband." I turned around.

Harold nodded. He looked expectantly at me. Harold always sees the good in people. He never has ill thoughts for anyone. "So what kind of folks are they?" he said.

"They're . . . different," I said. I turned back to the window. "They make kind of a different couple." I paused. I couldn't tell him everything because sometimes I have such thoughts, thoughts that surprise even myself, thoughts not fit to tell.

"What's he like?" Harold asked.

"Just a little fellow," I said. "And kind of a nervous type, too."

"Well, if he's a little skittish, that stands to reason," Harold said, crackling open his newspaper once again, glancing down the page. "Imagine yourself ending up in Washington, D.C."

"I know one thing."

"What's that?"

"They'll need some help getting squared away here. In our town," I said.

"So we'll help them. These things take time," Harold said in his faraway reading voice.

WINSTON SONNENFELD's cattle were due on Friday. He had called the telephone number of a cattle jockey in Des Moines, had ordered up two dozen Holsteins.

"The man wants cattle!" Harold said. "He's been up town every day and that's all he talks about—cattle."

Wednesday and Thursday, Harold and two other retired men helped Winston Sonnenfeld fix fence. Harold came home at noon with his shirt sweated through and barbed wire nicks like bright red bird feet on his wrists. He sat on the couch. He was breathing too fast.

"Don't try to do everything at once," I said. "Take it a little easier."

"If we don't get those wires up there'll be steers all over our cornfield," he said. He still called it "our" corn, though we rented out the land now. Harold leaned back on the couch.

"You better eat," I said. I had scalloped potatoes and ham ready. "Better get some food in your belly."

"A little later, maybe," he said. He stretched out his legs, slowly caught his breath.

"Does he help you? The doctor's husband?" I asked.

Harold looked out the window. "Some," he said. "He's . . . average, you could say. And not on the high side of average." He looked at me briefly, then lay back his head and let his eyes drift shut. His mouth slipped open and suddenly he was asleep.

I unfolded the afghan and walked over to Harold. For a moment I stared down at him, at the red scratches on his hands and wrists. They were like tiny roads on a map. I covered him, then looked out the west window toward the Whittier place. Beyond the cornfield was the windbreak, part of the white barn, the gray roofline of the house. The Whittier buildings seemed closer than I remembered. The Whittiers were a family of redheads, a whole flock of them, a poor family, none of them farmers, really. They left about 1950, silently, in the middle of the night. One morning they were gone. They left the machinery in the yard, the cattle in the barn, even pans on the stove and dishes on the table. Some said they went to California, others said Idaho. Nobody knew for sure. Even though the farm had changed hands several times since then, people still called it the Whittier place.

Why?

Sometimes I wanted to know the answer to that question. Why did their name stick when other names hadn't? Was it the flock of children, their red hair? Was it the unsettled accounts in town? Was it their cows bellowing for water in the barn? Their dishes still in the sink?

A CATTLE TRUCK rumbled past our house Friday at ten in the morning and turned into the Whittier place. Harold quickly pulled on his boots and found his gloves. He phoned the other men, and headed out the door.

"Be careful," I said.

He didn't hear me.

At lunchtime Harold's boots squeaked on the shoe scraper, a plow lay, sharp edge up, set in concrete. I'd always liked the sound.

"How'd it go?" I said.

"All right," he answered, "I guess." He was breathing hard again. He took off his cap. His forehead was white and sweaty above, dusty and streaked below, the red cap line in between. He left on his boots.

"You have to go back?" I asked.

"Should."

"Why?"

"Well," he said, dropping into a chair, "they're not steers. And they're not dehorned." He looked at me.

I was silent.

"Some bad horns in there," Harold explained. "Eight-, ten-

inchers. Razors. And they're all bulls, too. Those animals need
cutting on both ends."

"Why didn't the trucker say something before he came?" I
said.

"He said nobody asked him."

I was silent. Then I said, "Let the veterinarian handle it. The
Sonnenfelds can afford it. Doctors make good money."

"We can use my squeeze chute," Harold said. "I've got all
the equipment. It won't take but a couple of hours."

I turned away to the sink.

"I think it would mean a lot to them," Harold said.

AFTER LUNCH I went along to the Whittier place. I didn't like
the whole business. I wanted to be there.

The doctor's husband was perched on a corral post fence
watching his cattle. The animals milled around the lot, kicking
up dust, sniffing each other, then shying. They were bigger
than I had expected, long yearlings at least, seven or eight hundred pounds. A streak of blood ran down the black-and-white
flank of one animal.

We walked up to the doctor's husband. He was dressed in
jeans, a fresh white T-shirt, and new brown cowboy boots. A
smooth leather whip was coiled around his arm.

"Hello there," I called.

He didn't answer or turn. He was smiling at his cattle.

Behind us in the yard came two pickups with four men Harold knew, all white-haired, all retired farmers. They wore gloves
and boots. One carried the long dehorning pincers and a meat
saw. Another man carried a plastic bucket with some small
tools inside that clinked as he walked. The men explained
things to Winston, then set up the squeeze chute in the nar-
rowest part of the corral. When the chute was in place Winston
and the youngest of the white-haired men crawled through the
fence and began to walk the cattle forward.

"Hi-yahh!" Winston screamed.

"Easy does it!" the other man called.

The first bull ran straight into the chute. Harold slammed shut the rear gate and the man in front threw down the nose clamp. They had him. Harold started on the horns while the other leaned behind with a knife. The bull thrashed and bellowed and his hoofs rang on the iron and the whole chute shuddered. I was close enough to see the tiny fountains of blood come from the new red eyes on the skull. One vein threw a thin spray up and over Harold's shoulder. Blood pressure. So much pressure from the inside it was a wonder the skin could hold it back. Wind caught the little geyser of blood and spattered it onto Harold and onto the metal pipes and onto the other man, too.

"Needle-nose," Harold called. With the little pliers Harold caught the vein, rolled it once around the pincers, then pulled. The vein came out white and soft and stringy, a little spaghetti noodle. The blood stopped spurting. Steam came from the holes in the animal's skull, and through the holes, beneath a membrane, the brain moved. Then Harold sealed the holes with a quick smear of pine tar. The rear man sprayed Blue-Kote on the floppy scrotum. Then the gates swung wide and the steer lunged free.

"Hey," the doctor's husband said suddenly. He was staring at Harold, at the spatters of blood on Harold's shirt and face. "You hurt?"

"Not me," Harold said.

"He's the one hurting," one of the men said, and pointed to the steer which was now trotting in circles and shaking its head.

The other men laughed.

Winston Sonnenfeld walked slowly toward Harold. He squinted at the blood on Harold. Harold tried to see down his own nose; he wiped his cheeks with his right hand. The doctor's husband reached out to Harold's shirt and with a finger touched a spot of the blood.

The other men stared.

"We better run the next one in," Harold said, stepping away from Winston.

Winston looked down to the dehorner in Harold's hands.
"Can I try?" Winston asked.

Harold looked at the other men, then back. He shrugged.
"Sure," he said.

The next bull banged into the chute and was secured. Harold showed Winston the correct angle of the saw. "Cut too deep and they bleed," Harold said. "Cut too shallow and the horns grow back. You have to cut just deep enough to catch the horn root."

Winston sawed. The bull bellowed. The horn tipped sideways and a vein began to pulse and throw a red mist. The blood painted Winston's T-shirt.

"Step back—I'll pull that vein," Harold said.

After a pause Winston stepped slowly backwards. The spray of blood stitched red down his shirt, his pants.

"Just lean sideways next time," Harold said. "No sense getting wet."

Winston stared down at his clothes.

"Next—" Harold called.

On the next bull the doctor's husband again leaned into the blood and let it spatter on him. He kept doing that. I saw him. He kept leaning into the blood. By three o'clock the bulls were all steers and the doctor's husband looked as if he had been in some terrible car wreck or knife fight.

The men went to the barn's outside faucet and washed their arms and their faces. Winston followed. Harold stepped aside for Winston. Winston stared at the first men's clean faces, their shining, dripping arms. He looked at Harold's arms and hands.

"Sorry, got to go," Winston said suddenly. He checked his watch. "I just remembered, I'm supposed to meet Trudy in town."

"Don't go looking like that," Harold said. "Take a minute. Wash up."

"No time for that!" Winston said. He walked quickly to his car, started the engine, and drove away.

We stared after his cloud of dust.

"He looks like road kill," one of the men said.

"Why would he go to town looking like that?" another man said.

"He goes to the clinic like that, they'll think he's hurt bad," another said.

Harold stared down the road a long time. His forehead furrowed and for an instant something passed through his eyes, something quick and dark and ragged at its edges, like the shadow of a crow falling across a garden. Then he bent to the faucet, to its cold stream, and washed his hands. He kept turning and turning them, a long time, long after the pink water turned clear.

WHILE HAROLD napped I made up a big wild-rice hotdish. Over the years I've come to believe that certain farm jobs like dehorning, or the first spring plowing, or the last cornpicking, deserve something a little special. Otherwise, the weeks and the months and even the years just melt into one another. Melt together and slip away.

As I chopped celery I thought of the doctor herself. Of how difficult it must be for her having a man like that for a husband. I paused for a moment, then took out a second glass baking dish.

When the hotdishes came out of the oven, I put the best-looking one in a box, along with a jar of dills, little fancy dills with garlic cloves in the brine. I took the box and drove the quarter mile to the Whittier place.

Their car, a green foreign type that looked like a turtle, was parked right up by the house, on the grass. I parked back on the gravel and then walked forward. I carried the hotdish and the jar of pickles.

In the lot the steers huddled in one corner and waved their heads against the flies and thumped their hooves on the dirt to kick up dust.

I stepped onto the porch. I heard voices from inside. One loud voice and one voice whining like a child's. I raised my hand to knock and that's when I heard it. It was a sound I hadn't heard since I was child, since my brothers used to get in trouble with Father. I heard the flat crackling slap of a belt on bare skin. The high voice—the doctor's husband—called out, "Please! I'm sorry!"

Then she swore at him, words I've never used. Words I've never heard people use in Springfield. Words I've hardly ever read even in the newest paperbacks.

The belt cracked again.

My heart started to pound. I drew back my hand. The hot-dish was heavy in my arms, its breath hot and fishy. I felt faint. I backed away from the porch. I walked backwards all the way to the car.

When I got home Harold was still napping. I didn't wake him. So as not to disturb him I sat on the porch. I rocked and watched the sun sink toward the cornfield. As its bright ball neared the sharp tips of the corn I began to rock faster. I felt my blood pressure rising—heard a faint, faraway pump start up, felt my blood rising slow and steady like water crawling up the sides of a well.

I turned away from the sun and tried to breathe easily. I watched cars passing on the highway, but the sun was headed there, too. It burned through the posts and barbed wire and rolled exactly into the middle of the highway. Cars came and went from its red mouth. I closed my eyes against its light, and that's when I saw Doc Langenson's car.

I saw it pass our driveway that night. Its long, dark shape hurtled by without sound or lights—there was plenty of moonlight to drive by. Just beyond our mailbox the Cadillac swerved—a turn suddenly remembered—bounded across the ditch and soared deep into the body of the field.

I opened my eyes. I was breathing hard, rocking too fast. I kept my eyes open but still I saw things.

I saw the Whittier family. I saw them, in the moonlight, in silhouette, one by one sneaking down the steps of their house and crowding into their old car. I saw the car, headlights dark, ease out the driveway and turn west. I saw it shrink away, then vanish into the black landscape of the country.

Then I saw Doc Langenson's Cadillac again, coming backwards from the field, bursting into view, cornstalks falling away from the hood and trunk, corn jerking upright into straight and even rows like in a movie running backwards. I saw Doc's car regain the highway and back up fast—then its tires squealed in their braking. The Cadillac turned its long nose up our driveway, Harold's and mine, the Granlund place, where it had been heading all along. It picked up speed, its long fins gleaming, pulling dust and moonlight through the dark.

And I saw myself, in the last few moments before Doc arrived, trying to order my thoughts. Trying to think of everything left undone, unthought, unsaid.

But all that came into my head was those Whittier kids.

Not Fred Lynde.

Not Harold and the first day we met. Our wedding day, none of that.

I could think only of that red-haired Whittier family, of them leaving in the night. I wanted to know where they had gone, what had become of the children. I wanted to know what kind of people could walk away with food still on the table.

FROM THE LANDING

THE SUMMER I was seven years old and of no real use to my father—hay bales were too heavy, tractors too tall—my grandfather came almost daily to take me fishing. But whenever his gray Ford slowed at our driveway and its wheels crunched gravel in their turning, I ran away.

That July morning I ran to the garden, down its rows of sharp-leaved sweet corn, shielding my face with my arms, until I reached the shady center where the dirt was damp and cool. I hunkered there out of sight. In the yard my grandfather's Ford coasted to a halt; its engine sputtered and died.

In the silence pigeon feet scraped atop the metal dome of the silo. A calf bleated in the barn. Around me, mosquitos whined faintly like tiny, faraway planes taking off, as they rose up from the damp stalks and roots toward the heat of my body.

The Ford's horn tooted.

I squatted lower still, crouching there, hoping my grandfather would start his engine and drive away, drive up the road to my cousin Bobby's farm—take Bobby fishing, not me.

The Ford's radio came on. Music, some faint country-western song, began to play off the wide face of the barn and into the garden. Mosquitos lit on my ankles, my shoulders, my neck. I swore at them. I swore at the music, at old men who can wait all day—and again at the mosquitos, which finally drove me from my hiding place.

As I crossed the garden I picked up a hoe. I'd been working, hadn't heard my grandfather drive in. But the hoe was unnecessary, for behind the steering wheel my grandfather sat staring straight ahead through the windshield to the fields beyond; he didn't turn. Atop the Ford, three cane poles were tied to the roof. Three red and white bobbers, clipped to black lines, swayed slightly in a breeze I could not feel.

I came alongside the car.

"Hey, Buddy!" my grandfather said. His face lit up as if either he or I had been away somewhere, as if two days were a long time. He switched off the radio.

"Hi, Gramps," I said loudly.

He looked at the hoe. "What you digging, Buddy?"

"Hoeing," I said. "It's not a shovel, it's a hoe." I held it up close to his face. He leaned forward. His watery blue eyes squinted first at the hoe, then across to the garden.

"Finished?" he asked.

"Supposed to do four more rows," I said.

He blinked at the garden. "Those weeds will be there tomorrow," he said. "Right now we better pick up Bobby and go, else our minnows will die."

My cousin Bobby lived on the next farm south, but he was nowhere to be seen. I searched our bale forts in the hayloft. I peered inside the empty calf hutches beside the dairy barn. I eased into the silo room and squinted between the vinegary-smelling stacks of wooden doors. I slipped into the milk house and sprang behind the big stainless-steel bulk tank. No Bobby.

Back in the yard I paused for a moment to look around. Some scruffy white hens were easing back to their sand-scratching spot in front of the machine shed; they kept clucking and looking around. I circled behind the building to the scrap-iron pile. I slowed among the junked cornpickers, the half-combines, the black piles of old tires. I found Bobby curled up inside an old tractor tire like one white bean in a big black pod. I leaned into the tire and grinned down at him. "Grandpa's here," I said.

"Double-damn!" he shouted. His voice circled inside the tire and came at me from behind. It sounded like his father's voice. Bobby was a year older than me. He had blond hair like me but was thicker in his chest and shoulders, and sometimes he got to drive the little Allis-Chalmers tractor all by himself.

Bobby scrambled out of the tire. He went to the corner of the machine shed and peeked around it into the yard. "Damn," he whispered. He looked back at me and folded his arms across his chest. "I ain't going," he said.

I shrugged.

The Ford's horn tooted.

"You better tell Grandpa, then," I said.

Bobby was silent. "You tell him for me." He stepped one step toward me and raised a fist. "Tell him you couldn't find me," Bobby said.

I shook my head no.

Bobby stared at me; he lowered his fist.

"I'll let you drive the Allis," he said.

I thought about that for a while. Then I shook my head no.

He raised his fist again.

I closed my eyes and braced myself.

Bobby swore again.

When I opened my eyes he was staring back toward the yard.

The horn tooted again.

Bobby turned to look at me. For a long moment we stared at each other—then we broke for the yard. Dust flew, chickens scattered as we ran, but Bobby beat me to the back seat and slammed the door and locked it. I had to sit in front.

"Ready, boys?" Grandpa said.

"Sure," Bobby called from the back. He giggled, then hissed in my ear. "I'll come to your funeral. I'll sit in the first pew, but there won't be no open casket."

"I wouldn't even come to yours," I said. "Nobody will."

"Nobody's who's dead already, you mean," Bobby said.

"Shut up," I said. We spoke without turning our heads or moving our lips.

Grandpa brought up the RPMs and let out the clutch. The Ford jerked ahead.

"Christ, he started in third!" Bobby said.

"So third is better than reverse," I said.

The Ford swung wide onto the lawn, then found gravel again, and we were on our way. Across the driveway a yellow oat field stretched away west; midfield, between windrows of grain, two pickups sat parked beside the red Massey-Ferguson grain swather. The swather's reel stood high in the air like an upraised aluminum fist: breakdown. My father and my uncle Karl lay under the swather with only their legs sticking out. On the yellow oat stubble the swather was a big hub and their legs were the spokes of a broken wheel.

The Ford drew even with the field. Grandpa didn't notice the machinery or the pickups, and the men on the ground did not look out toward the road.

"Crappies are biting over on Boulder Lake, boys," Grandpa said.

"Triple-damn," Bobby groaned. "You know what that means," he said in my ear.

I knew. The highway.

"You coulda told him you couldn't find me," Bobby said. He kicked the seat hard from behind.

Grandpa felt the kick. He turned. "Boys!" he said. "Steady now." Then he looked back to the road. He drove with his head tilted back, his arms straight out to the steering wheel. "Crappies big as dinner plates," he said in his faraway driving voice.

WE DROVE on gravel, and as we neared the highway I began to watch Grandpa's eyes and the stop sign swimming up red. His eyes kept staring straight on down the road. I put my hands on the dashboard. Finally I said, "Stop sign, Gramps."

With his right hand Grandpa lifted his leg onto the brake. The Ford came to a halt with a scrape of gravel on asphalt. I let out a breath. The Ford's front bumper hung on the white center stripe, and a passing motor home swung wide and tooted its horn. A wall of air rocked the Ford.

"You want me to take the front seat?" Bobby said.

"Why? What's the matter?" I said. I grinned out of Bobby's sight, and he swore again.

Grandpa waited at the intersection. "Say when, Buddy," he said to me.

THE CRAPPIES schooled but were not hungry. Our three white bobbers swam sideways, then in small circles, but never dipped beneath the surface. Bobby and I gave up casting and fished straight over the side of the boat. We took turns threading minnows onto Grandpa's hook; it took him so long, bent over the hook and minnow like he was sewing something, that we helped him so we didn't have to watch.

"Okay," Bobby said, and swung Grandpa's baited hook out and away from us. Bobby checked his wristwatch and looked at the sun. He looked at me. I looked away, toward my bobber. It was moving away from the boat, toward the landing. I set the hook hard but there was nothing there.

"Tomorrow," Grandpa said to us, "they'll bite tomorrow."

ON THE WAY home Bobby had to take the front seat, and I lay full length in the back. The rear seat was deep and soft and scratchy and smelled like dog. I watched the green tops of spruce trees flash by the window, then change to blue sky as we turned onto the highway. I smelled water as we passed a swamp, pigs from a farm.

Bobby's side of the seat tilted back an inch. "A little more to the right, Gramps," Bobby said.

A big semitrailer's air horn blasted over us and its slipstream shuddered the Ford.

Bobby let out a breath and swore again.

I didn't look up. By the passing smells and the flow of tree-tops against blue sky I kept track of where we were. Two more miles. I closed my eyes.

"Curve," Bobby said to Grandpa. I felt Bobby's seat tilt back again.

I kept my eyes closed until the Ford slowed and gravel chattered in the wheel wells. Bobby whirled in his seat and punched me hard in the chest.

"What'd you do that for!" I said. It hurt.

Bobby grinned down at me. "Just for the hell of it," he said. He kept grinning down at me.

"Watch the damn road," I said.

"Hey, made in the shade!" Bobby replied. Then he said, "You shoulda seen that semi—a big Peterbilt with a flat front. I swear it was big as a barn!" He spread his fingers and pushed his open palm straight at my face.

I swatted his hand away. "We're not home yet," I said, "you'd better—"

Suddenly the Ford scraped and tilted. So fast. When we hit I went onto the floor, onto the minnow pail, and I felt rocks slamming underneath, grating on the muffler and tailpipe. Bobby shouted and I saw his arms grab for the wheel. Then we were stopped.

There was silence. Crappie minnows flipped and twisted in a pool of water on the floor. My shirt was wet.

"Boys," Grandpa said slowly, "what have we done?"

He began to open his door.

"No—not that side," Bobby shouted.

I peeked up out of my window on the driver's side. The Ford hung on the slanted shoulder of the road. Below were cattails and water in the ditch. I scrambled to the high side of the Ford.

"This way, Gramps!" I shouted close to his ear. We pulled him over to Bobby's seat.

Grandpa squinted out his window. I knew he could see only sky. "Boys—we got too far over," he murmured.

Bobby and I looked at each other. Bobby began to giggle. I did, too.

"Somebody better go for help," Grandpa said.

"Me!" Bobby said immediately. He eased out his door,

dropped to the ground, then sprinted off down the road. His tennis shoes kicked up dust. Bobby's dust hung in the sunlight even when he was out of sight over the hill, like part of him had stayed behind.

THIRTY MINUTES later a pickup came fast down the road. My father drove. Bobby rode standing up in the rear. I waited outside the car, and soon the truck braked hard, its dust rolling over me and then onto the Ford, where Grandpa waited. The men and Bobby hurried forward. A smudge of oil streaked my father's forehead. He wore dark green, dusty coveralls with some silvery box-end wrenches jammed in the front pockets; the wrenches clanked as he walked and their dark eyes swayed.

"What the hell happened here?" my father said. He looked at the car, then at my grandfather, who had remained in the front seat, on the passenger's side.

Grandpa was silent for a moment. "Cut it too wide, I guess," he said slowly.

"He can't drive worth a damn anymore," Bobby said, jerking his head at Grandpa. I waited for my uncle to nail Bobby for swearing, but nothing happened. Though none of us stirred, I felt Bobby take some kind of step away from me. Or me from him. One of us moved.

"He almost killed Buddy and me!" Bobby said. "Every time we go with him he almost kills us."

No one said anything.

My father turned to stare at me. Then he looked at his own father, then back to me.

"Buddy?" my father asked.

I looked down. I shrugged. "We got too far over, that's all."

"Hell, that's not all—" Bobby said. "Today we almost got hit by a motor home, then by a semi. If we didn't help him drive he couldn't drive at all!"

My grandfather stared at Bobby. He was reading Bobby's lips. Bobby looked straight at him. Bobby's face was red and he swallowed, but he still kept staring straight on.

My father turned to me. "How long has this been going on?" he said slowly.

I looked down.

"Buddy?" my father repeated.

"What been going on?" I said.

"You helping him drive."

Bobby answered for me. "All this summer. Most of last summer, too."

My father knelt to look at me straight on. "Buddy, you should have said something," he said. He looked up to his own brother, my uncle. "We get busy, I know, but still you should have told us." His face had gone white.

I looked down. My eyes and throat burned. The shapes around me—the truck, my father, small stones on the road, the silver eyelets on my own boots—wavered and swelled and shimmered. I wiped my eyes.

Uncle Karl turned to my grandfather. "Well, the damn fishing trips are over. If you can't drive on the right side of the road, you shouldn't be driving at all."

My grandfather stared a long time at the men, at Bobby. Then he leaned over and removed the ignition keys. He stared at them in his hand for a moment, then slowly held them out the window. The keys caught sunlight as they fell.

YEARS LATER I saw Bobby and his wife only occasionally. Bobby had stayed home to take over his father's place and two of my other uncles' farms. There was not enough land for everybody to farm, but that was all right by me. I was a teacher by then and I lived a hundred miles away with my own wife and kids. I came back to the farm three or four times a year to help my father put up wood or just to walk the fence lines and look for birds and animal tracks. I always brought my children along; I wanted them to know what a farm was like without their having to live on one.

Those trips back were when I saw Bobby. We didn't have much in common anymore, only the past, so once a year, usually in July, we went fishing together. We took Bobby's boat down to Little Moon, the lake closest to the farm. No weekend trip to Canada, nothing like that. Just one evening on a lake.

On one of those evenings, Bobby's chores ran late and the sun was already low and orange before we pushed off from the landing. The lake was a plate of blue. Disturbed, the water around the boat gave off a chill and a reedy smell, but the sun was warm on my neck and shoulders. Across the lake two loons swam just beyond the reed point where the water dropped off.

Bobby didn't start up the Evinrude. He rowed, and then we drifted and we fished the shoreline. We sat at opposite ends of the boat and cast shiner minnows toward the bank, then jigged them slowly toward deep water. The minnows wavered, glinting, across green moss, then blue water, then broke through to daylight and air where they spun off bright droplets as we cast them again.

Bobby and I didn't talk much. On a lake at sundown with a rod and reel in your hands, there wasn't much that needed saying.

Two mallards came in low and set their wings.

Bobby said, "Old Gramps would have dropped those two."

"You've got that right," I said.

We cast again.

Then Bobby said something about Grandpa's Winchester twelve-gauge, and we got to talking more. We spoke about that gun. About the old Allis-Chalmers. The '39 Ford.

We fell silent for a few casts. The air and water blued toward each other.

Then Bobby said, "Sometimes I think old Gramps might still be fishing."

I didn't know quite what he meant. "Maybe so," I said.

We cast again.

"If it weren't for me, he'd still be fishing," Bobby said. "That's what I meant."

I was silent.

"That day when we got off too far with the Ford," Bobby said. His back was to me.

"I remember that day," I said. I chuckled once. Bobby didn't laugh.

He reeled his minnow up from the water, and sat staring at it for a long time. A clear bead of water stretched from the tail of his minnow.

"He never drove his car after that day," Bobby said.

I didn't say anything.

"He just sat there in his chair in his living room and shriveled up and died," Bobby said.

I slowed my reeling.

Bobby turned to me. "Sometimes I think I killed him," Bobby said softly. "That was the day I killed my own grandfather."

"That's crazy," I said. "You don't want to think that."

Bobby kept staring at me, but beyond me as well. Then he shook his head and focused his eyes on me. "Nothing is crazy," he said. "Everything is crazy and nothing is crazy."

We stared at each other for a long moment. I was the one who looked away. I felt Bobby's eyes on me, then we cast our minnows at the same time. That's when I began to talk. I felt it was my duty. I told Bobby that somebody had to say it, how our grandfather was endangering us and everybody else on the road; how the driving couldn't have gone on forever.

At first Bobby was silent. Occasionally he nodded. After a while he said things like "Maybe so," or "I guess I can see that."

The air shaded from blue to purple. We kept casting, and slowly Bobby began to talk, at first about our grandfather, then, slowly, about other things. I talked, too. As we cast our minnows into the shortening light, the shrinking depth of field, with each swing of our arms we threw off some thin layer of our bodies until an hour later only our voices were left in the dark. After that we fished by the faint, reflected starlight, by the habits of our hands.

We spoke of our kids.

Our jobs.

Our wives.

Our jobs again.

Things we wanted to do with our lives but hadn't done. Bobby said he had always wanted to go to Alaska and catch a king salmon. "Just one king salmon would do it," he told me.

I said I wanted to go to Brazil, to Rio de Janeiro and the Carnival there. I wanted to wear one of those tall costumes and dance the samba.

Bobby laughed at that, and so did I.

Everything there was to say about ourselves, that night we said it. We only stopped talking when one or the other of us cast—when the brief whistle of a rod split the air. We paused as line whispered off the reel, clear monofilament line reaching into the dark, unwinding to a moment of silence just before the minnow, somewhere far out there, kissed down on water.

We fished until car lights angled yellow through the trees and bounced sharply toward the landing. The beams cast their light onto the water, then halted. A car door slammed. Someone moved between the beams, one of our wives, we couldn't tell which one, and began to call out for us. Our names came across the water, then again in echo from the dark shore behind. Someone from the landing stood there calling to us, asking were we still out there? Were we all right?

THE COWMAN

One green June morning, Wayne Moen, Sr., a broad-shouldered man with ruddy cheeks, did not come in from the dairy barn. His wife found him facedown between two cows. The Holsteins had swung wide in their stanchions and kicked at the milking machines still pulsing on their teats. In town that week when people discussed the sudden death of Wayne Moen, Sr.—he was only fifty-five—the subject of the milking machines inevitably came up. How long had those milkers been on the two cows? What would that do to an udder?

For Wayne Moen, Jr., and his mother there was a larger question: what to do with the fifty dairy cows? Wayne Jr., an only child, less stocky than his father but similarly red-cheeked and balding, lived two hundred miles away in Minneapolis. After high school Wayne had farmed one year with his father. There was not enough income for two, however, and his father had not wanted to build a larger dairy barn, rent more land. There had been words. Wayne left for the Twin Cities. For the last eleven years he had worked in Blaine, a northern suburb, at Xytronics, a plastic injection-molding plant where he was now Trim Foreman. The job had overtime, insurance, a retirement package if he could hang on that long. His wife, Judy, also worked. She sold Amway full-time, was a district distributor shooting for regional. They had no children. But when Wayne's mother called that June morning, he and Judy dropped everything and drove north. Wayne had two weeks of vacation he'd been saving for the fishing opener, but who could think of fishing now?

In the two days before the funeral, Wayne struggled with the chores. The cows shied from his hands. He woke up too early. He was stiff. He could think only of naps. At mealtimes he ate like a spring bear, enormous plates of Swiss steak or waffles and eggs or hotdishes and bread, and was constipated. He felt groggy, felt underwater. Luckily Judy was there to help his mother with the cooking, with the visitors, with the open house after the funeral.

The day following the funeral, Judy returned to Blaine. She had to keep track of her Amway girls, keep them moving. "Otherwise, they'll just sit down," she said. After Judy was gone, Wayne realized he had hardly spoken with his wife for days. But he couldn't be blamed for that. Not under the circumstances.

Alone, Wayne slept in his old bedroom upstairs under the eaves. The roof sloped sharply over his bed, and once in the night raindrops drummed sharply just above his face. He sat up in bed and did not know how old he was. His room was the same. A buck's head hung on the wall; a frilly pink garter dangled from the black horns. The garter was Milly Hortner's, a large girl with sharp perfume, and whose pubic hair Wayne had touched (when? last night? years ago?); the coarseness of her hair, like the bristles of a curry comb, had surprised him and he'd jerked away his hand. On the bulletin board were newspaper clippings, bone-colored on dark cork. A small round mirror. There was no clock. Wayne switched on the light and checked his watch. The time. The date. He rose and went to the small mirror by the doorway and peered into it. Patches of the dark backing had peeled away to clear glass and he could see only a part of his face at one time.

An eye.

A mouth.

A chin.

A balding forehead, his father's forehead. In that moment Wayne felt his body settle into its rightful age: thirty.

On the seventh morning home, Wayne slept until the alarm rang. When he swung his legs from bed their stiffness was gone. After chores he ate breakfast, a single egg with toast and black coffee, and felt full. He was alert, ready for the day. It was 8:00 A.M. and he was free to choose his work. He could look through the Holsteins' breeding records. He could cultivate corn. Or he could drive to town and drink coffee. He was free. Free, of course, until the evening milking, but that was twelve hours away.

Wayne looked at the kitchen clock and saw through it to Xytronics back in Blaine. He saw his friend Dan, saw "Dickhead" Gaskins, the manager, and all the other saps just now stumbling into work, feeding quarters into the coffee machine, waiting for those paper cups with the sharp-edged cardboard handles, stirring in packets of chemical creamer. And behind everything the faint stink of hot plastic.

"Another egg?" Wayne's mother said.

Wayne shook his head no.

"Bacon, then,"

"Nope, full."

"Toast, surely?"

Wayne grinned. "Full, Mom. Full."

She turned away to the sink.

He watched her for a moment. With her back to him, she looked up at the wall. "Maybe then we should talk about the cows," she said quietly.

They sat at the kitchen table. "First," Wayne said, "we could sell them."

Wayne's mother looked down at her hands. "An auction?" she murmured. Then she looked out the window, toward the barn. The quick shadow of a frown passed through her eyes; Wayne saw cars and pickups parked on the lawn, saw the auctioneer, saw cattle trailers, saw white Styrofoam cups littering the yard, people fishing in the trash barrels for aluminum cans.

"Not necessarily an auction," Wayne said. "A cattle jockey would buy the whole herd."

"Where would the cows go?" she said, turning back to Wayne.

Wayne sipped his coffee.

"Would the herd stay together?"

Wayne was silent.

His mother turned again to look out the window. "He had thirty years of breeding in those cows," she said.

Wayne poured himself more coffee.

"Second, we could lease the herd to some other farmer," Wayne said. "Maybe there's a younger dairyman who would—"

"Not that," his mother said immediately. "Those younger farmers, they milk three times a day. They use weekend milking help, kids from town who don't know anything about cows. The young farmers take regular vacations, like having cows was some sort of . . . corporation. They push too hard, they burn out their cows like they burn up plow lays in dry ground," she said. As she spoke her voice deepened and slowed, and she finished in Wayne's father's voice. She turned suddenly to Wayne. Her eyes were wide and scared.

Wayne stood up and held her. His mother's shoulders began a slow, silent heaving, and he held her a long time. He stared past the white cloud of her hair through the open window and into the yard. The red barn stood with its wide-faced, open gaze. Below and to the side the cows lazily bumped each other around the water tank. Sunlight shone on their flanks and on the dust they swung into the air with their tails. Beyond the cows was the cornfield his father had planted, its straight rows disappearing east into a haze of green. Into this scene no one came and no one went.

"What the hell," Wayne said softly, hearing the words as if he were outside his own body. "I'll take over the cows. Judy and me."

A YEAR LATER, in the same month of June, Wayne stood in his father's barn beside the heifer. She rocked in her stanchion side to side, leg to leg. Wayne ran his hand down the black-and-white swell of her belly. She was six days overdue. The calf inside shifted, then kicked against Wayne's hand; for an instant her belly grew horns and the heifer shuddered. Then the points retracted, the skin smoothed and the heifer resumed her rocking motion.

"Lie the hell down," Wayne muttered. He rapped her rear hocks with his boot, tried to spread her legs, but the heifer flung a hind leg at him; the hoof grazed his shin and he stumbled backwards.

"Stand there then, dammit," he said without heat. He reached up for the light bulb's string.

Crossing from barn to house in the gray dark before dawn, Wayne ruled out returning to bed. Judy would wake up, and anyway, it was already 4:30 A.M. Milking was only an hour away. On the porch he quietly removed his boots, then slipped inside. In the living room the couch and two easy chairs glowed pale blue under their sheets. One large and two smaller mushrooms of light, a spare fairy ring. When Judy had moved from Minneapolis to the farm she covered all the living-room furniture with bed sheets so it would not smell like cows. Wayne lay down. Before closing his eyes he turned his face to the side and lifted a corner of the sheet. There was a pattern, large swirls of leaves and vines. Black flowers. He waited, but could not recall their real color. He lay back. As he stared at the ceiling he realized, too, that he had crossed from barn to house without once looking at the sky. He did not know if the night was overcast or starry.

At 5:30 A.M., as a fist of pink was rising in the dark blue eastern sky, Wayne walked in the footpath to the barn. The path was a faint, narrow channel worn, over the years, by his father's feet. It was like a dead furrow in an old pasture, hard to see but easily felt beneath a tractor tire or one's own boots, a path jolting to cross, easy to follow. As he walked in the path, sometimes Wayne's legs and feet felt strange. Felt light. Felt ahead of themselves. Felt as if the trunk of his body were in danger of falling behind. When this sensation occurred,

Wayne immediately left the path and walked on harder dirt.

On the path was not the only time Wayne felt the lightness. Sometimes, working with a fork or a shovel, its handle worn smooth by his father's labor, Wayne's own hands tingled. Felt gone. In the tractor's seat Wayne often felt the contours of his father's thighs and legs; and his own legs felt lost. Whenever this lightness came upon him, Wayne altered his grip or moved his hands or shifted his body, and the feeling soon enough went away.

Inside the barn, Wayne approached the heifer. She stood braced against her stanchion, her tail arched over a slick red balloon the size of a baby's head. Wayne hurried closer. He peered into the membrane, looking for the shadow of the calf's hooves, but the balloon was empty. Briefly he stroked the heifer's spine, then turned to the other cows, to the milking.

An hour later Wayne rinsed the hot milkers with cold water. Then he ran a deep basin of warm water, added soap and a capful of chlorine, scrubbed the stainless steel tub with the various brushes. After the washing Wayne ran a hand inside the hot curves of the milkers, his fingers feeling for the faint, sandpapery grit of milkstone. Finding none, he sprayed the milkers with cold water and racked them on the wall. Last, with a hose he sprayed down the milk house floor. Bits of straw chaff whirled yellow in smaller and smaller circles, then disappeared down the black eye of the floor drain. He hurried back to the heifer.

Her membrane was the size of a basketball, and pale pink from its stretching. But nothing showed inside.

Wayne went to the house for breakfast.

IN THE KITCHEN Judy stood in her bathrobe at the stove scraping yellow eggs back and forth across a black skillet. "So how's your cow," she said without turning.

Heifer. A cow had already had a calf. But he imagined they were all just cows to her. He hoped that would change one day.

"She's starting," Wayne said. He made his voice cheerful. "She'll come in some time this morning."

Judy's spatula paused in mid-scrape. "Dan and Ellen and the twins will be here this morning," she said. She turned to Wayne. Her brown hair, chocolate beauty-shop brown, hung in two rollers, one on each side of her white face like two round, extra eyes. For a moment Wayne stared. The woman was a stranger. She was in the wrong house. The woman by the stove should be fully dressed, have gray hair tied up in back, a few white strands drifting down the sides. She should be smiling, holding out to him a steaming mug of coffee.

But now Wayne's mother lived in an apartment in town, had for nearly a year.

"Dan and Ellen, sure," Wayne said. When Judy turned back to the stove he glanced at the calendar.

Dan and Ellen, their friends from Minneapolis. From Xytronics.

"Well, I hope your cow goes fast," Judy said, scraping the eggs onto Wayne's plate. The spatula paused. "I suppose the twins could watch," she said. "They're eight now. I'm sure they've never seen a calf being born. It would be educational."

"Maybe," Wayne said. He sat and slid his chair toward the table. He sat where his father always sat. At the squeak of chair legs on linoleum, Wayne looked briefly to the window, to his own face in the glass.

"Sure. Why not?" Wayne said, surprised by the volume of his voice.

Judy looked briefly at him.

"The twins could watch," Wayne said. "It might do them good." He turned in his chair so he could see Judy while he ate. He talked to her. He asked her things. What she planned to do with Ellen. About the weather. About the twins. He ate and he made himself say things and listened carefully to the sound of his voice in this kitchen.

AFTER BREAKFAST, Wayne returned to the barn. The heifer's membrane sagged over the tips of two wet, white hooves. Big hooves. The heifer remained standing, rocking side to side.

"Lie down, damn you," Wayne said, tapping at her hind

hooves with his boot. The heifer lashed back at him with a hoof.

He brought around the calving board and lay it across the gutter. In the milk house he ran a pail of hot water, added a few drops of chlorine and a tablespoon of powdered soap. The soap foamed up in a white, crackling drift that flowed over the side. From the wall Wayne removed the stainless steel calving chains and dropped them into the bucket. They clanked out of sight on the metal bottom of the pail. He carried the bucket into the barn, poured half of the soapy water over the gutter-board, then brought around a fresh bale of straw and sat down on it.

The straw bale radiated heat and warmed his legs. After a few minutes he leaned back against the barn wall and folded his arms. He let his eyes drift shut. He listened to the cows chewing, shifting. Their sea rhythm.

"HEY, FARMERBOY!" someone was calling.

Wayne blinked and looked up. Someone moving black against the bright light of the east barn window. Some large shape moving toward him, reaching out its hand.

"Hey, farmer—no wonder you left the big city! Up here you can sleep on the job!"

Dan.

"Dan," Wayne said. He stood up from the bale, shaking his head, trying to wake up. The heifer shied from Dan's voice and tried to suck back the hooves of the calf.

"You made it," Wayne said. Behind Dan were Ellen and the twins. Wayne smelled cigarette smoke on Dan, perfume on Ellen. Behind their mother the blond-haired twins stepped carefully along the far wall, keeping their distance from the gutter. Dan was sandy-haired, wore a bushy beard, and carried a belly. Ellen was thin and sharp-edged; she plucked her eyebrows, then drew them back in higher arcs with brown pencil. Wayne had always thought of her as bony and unlubricated; he could not imagine her in bed.

"Look at the poop!" one of the twins said.

"Gross!" the other said.

Ellen and Dan laughed.

The heifer shied again.

"Hello, girls," Wayne said softly. He could never tell the twins apart so made no attempt at their names.

"Hi," they said in unison, still staring into the gutter, inching along.

"Calf coming?" Dan said.

Wayne nodded and turned to the heifer.

"Girls, come here, this is the mommy—" Ellen called. She stepped closer to look, and held on to Dan's arm. The heifer swung her rear end as far as she could from Ellen's voice.

The girls' eyes widened. "And we get to watch everything. You said we could!"

"Well, let's ask Wayne first," Ellen said.

Wayne paused. "It might take a while," Wayne said. At that moment the heifer bellowed and pushed against the calf's hooves. Ellen jumped back. The girls each grabbed onto one of Dan's legs. The calf's hooves strained outward to the white hair of their hocks, then sucked back. The girls stared, open-mouthed.

"Girls?" Ellen asked.

"Yuck!" one of them said.

"No, I want to watch," the other insisted.

"If it's okay with Wayne . . ." Ellen said.

Wayne shrugged. "Sure," he said.

"Me, I'm going up to the house," Ellen said with a fake grimace, "I don't need a lesson on how that's done."

Dan grinned at Wayne.

As Ellen left, Dan started to speak but the heifer bellowed again. For a moment Wayne glimpsed the white forelegs. They were thick. Too thick. A big bull calf.

"What say?" Wayne said.

"Your mom, she doing okay in town?"

"Fine," Wayne replied, which was mostly true.

"She's out here a lot, I'll bet," Dan said.

"No," Wayne said. "She says that's the hard part."

Dan nodded. He looked around the barn. "Jesus, that was something, when you think about it. Your dad here one day, gone the next."

Wayne was silent.

"What's it like being back?" Dan said. "I mean, where you were raised. Living in the same house."

"It's . . . different," Wayne said.

"I'll bet," Dan said.

Wayne turned to Dan. "Sometimes it's strange," he said slowly, "sometimes I feel like I'm sixteen or something and—"

"Sixteen!" Dan said. He grinned.

"Sixteen and my parents are gone for the weekend and I've got a girl staying over night."

"Young chick or older woman?" Dan said.

Wayne frowned, puzzled.

"I mean, does Judy get younger too, or stay thirty?"

Wayne thought a moment. "Stays thirty," he said.

"What the hell," Dan grinned. "A good-looking older woman."

Wayne smiled briefly.

The heifer bleated again and pushed, without progress, against the hooves.

Dan turned to Wayne. "So when you and Judy gonna drop one of your own?" he said with a wink.

Wayne was silent.

"Up here on the farm and all, I figured you guys would get in the swing of things, make a bunch of little farmhands," Dan said.

Wayne shrugged. "I don't know," he said. "From what the doc says, it looks like we might have to hire them instead."

Dan fell silent.

They looked at the heifer.

"Shit," Dan said, "I didn't know. Me and my trap," he said.

"Hey, don't worry about it," Wayne said. "I'm not."

Dan nodded.

They were silent again.

"Anyway," Dan said, turning to look around the barn, "I'd

have done the same thing. Come back home, I mean," he said. "Think about it. At the plant you've got the dickhead breathing down your neck; here, you're in charge. At the plant they're laying people off the line, then adding them upstairs; here, hell—you got a job for life!"

The heifer flinched at Dan's voice.

Wayne nodded but didn't reply. They talked some more, mainly about the plant. Xytronics had gotten a piece of the Masters of the Universe business, a molding contract for a laser lance and a wrist shield for one of the characters. Dan could not remember the name. "Either Skeletor or Randor." Xytronics had hired seven more trimmers. Wayne talked about milk and cattle prices, the hay crop. Soon they fell silent.

"Well, maybe I'll go up and get a cup of coffee," Dan said. "See what the ladies are up to."

"Sure. Okay," Wayne said.

"The girls won't be in the way?"

"No problem," Wayne said.

Dan nodded, and patted the girls on their heads.

WAYNE FOUND the twins a bale of straw. The girls sat down and leaned against each other. In the new silence the heifer began, again, at regular intervals, to push. The twins leaned forward, drew back, leaned forward with each contraction. Wayne slipped out of his coverall top and tied the sleeves around his waist. He washed his hands and wrists and arms in the warm water.

Push.

The calf's tongue, purple like a slice of liver, appeared between the white legs.

Push.

Wayne saw the black tip of its nose. He slipped the silvery chains around the calf's hooves, and cinched them tight, got ready. With the heifer's next push, Wayne pulled with her; she bawled and tried to scramble away, but Wayne gained the calf's nose. He kept tension on the chains. The heifer dropped her head to pant.

Wayne remembered to turn and smile at the twins. They sat welded together, white-faced, staring.

The heifer arched to push again. Wayne pulled again. She bellowed and shied.

In this way they worked.

After a half hour the chains began to deaden Wayne's arms. He looped twine through the chains and then around his back. When he pulled again, the rope chafed thin and hot across his spine—but the calf's head slid free. A white, horselike head. The calf's face wagged wildly side to side. Its tongue slurped for air.

Wayne readied himself for the final pull. When the heifer arched again, Wayne bent into the chains and the calf slid forward, long and white—to its hips. Wayne swore and braced harder into the chain. The heifer bawled and tried to pull back the calf. The calf flailed, a wet heavy pendulum sucking for the air, bleating. Wayne heaved against the chains, arching with the heifer. The calf's baa-ing weakened.

Wayne threw down the chains and tried to slide his hand alongside the calf and into the heifer but there was no room—bone against bone. The calf now hung straight down. Wayne grabbed the wet hair and swung the calf's face up to his own. Its lips were slick and salty as he began to blow air into the calf's mouth, deep lungfuls of his own breath into the calf. The calf's eyes stared straight on at his own eyes. He blew and blew until red pinwheels turned and milkweed pods shimmered away seeds of light and he had to hang on to the heifer to keep from falling—and he kept blowing even as the light in the calf's eyes dulled and flattened like a ground fog rising at sundown, slowly pushing the light back over the horizon until the sky turned gray.

Suddenly the barn tilted and Wayne sat down hard on the concrete. When his vision cleared, the calf was dead.

He stumbled to his feet swearing, a long hoarse cursing, the worst words—when he remembered the twins. He turned quickly to speak. Their straw bale was empty.

AN HOUR LATER the veterinarian came. He was an older man with thin, yellowing hair who had been Wayne's father's vet as well. Without speaking he shrugged on black rubber coveralls. There were tire patches here and there. Wayne remembered the coveralls, but there were more patches on them now. From his truck the vet brought a plastic pail and a meat saw with a rounded nose. Wayne saw him to the heifer where the calf hung like an extra tail.

"Big devil," were the vet's first words.

"Too big," Wayne said.

The vet nodded to Wayne with a brief glance containing a kind of recognition, the faraway beginning of a smile, the possibility of respect. Then he turned to spray disinfectant on his hands. His wrists. His arms. On the saw blade.

When it was over, Wayne walked slowly to the house.

"MY HUSBAND, the cowman," Judy announced as he came in.

They were all in the living room, Judy and Dan and Ellen and the kids. The sheets were off the furniture; orange flowers, yellow leaves. The twins, one each, sat on their parent's laps. When Wayne came into the room they looked down.

Dan and Ellen and Judy stared at him.

"Why did you let the girls stay?" Judy said. Her voice was soft, overly pleasant.

Wayne shrugged. "Things went bad. I forgot they were there."

"You forgot," Judy said. Her brown hair was curved and fluffy. She had on blue eye makeup and a dress that Wayne hadn't seen for a long time. She looked as if she was going somewhere. "Of course, he forgot," Judy said, turning to Dan and Ellen. "My husband, the cowman, he forgot."

THAT EVENING toward the end of supper, Ellen said to Judy, "Dan and I probably should be heading back."

"Back?" Judy said. "Tonight?"

Dan turned to look at Ellen.

"Gaskins might be calling Dan to work," Ellen said.

"Tonight?" Dan asked.

"Tomorrow," Ellen said.

"Tomorrow's Sunday," Dan said.

Ellen stared at Dan; she narrowed her lips.

Dan shrugged. "It's happened before, I guess," he said. He reached for his coffee.

"Well, let's have dessert, anyway," Judy said.

They ate pie and ice cream in silence until Judy turned to Ellen. "Maybe I'll ride down to Minneapolis with you," Judy said. She didn't look at Wayne.

No one spoke.

Dan and Ellen turned to Wayne.

"Sure," Ellen said, looking at Wayne. "If you want to ride along, that's fine."

"I might stay for a few days. Look around," Judy said.

"You're welcome at our house," Ellen said. "Right, Dan?"

Dan was silent. He looked at Wayne, "You're welcome, one or both of you, sure, anytime," he said. "Be more fun with the both of you, but you know us. Open house, anytime."

Later, with the girls and the women already in the car, the trunk lid up, Dan swung Judy's suitcases inside. Two large suitcases. Dan turned to Wayne. "Let me tell you I don't feel right about this. I'm not in favor of this," he said.

"None of it is on you," Wayne answered.

Dan was silent.

"This is between her and me," Wayne said.

"All right," Dan said. He let the trunk lid come down. Latched it. "I just wanted you to know."

"Now I know," Wayne said. He smiled at Dan.

They shook hands, and Dan kept pumping Wayne's hand.

"Hey—it's okay," Wayne said.

Dan grinned briefly and let go of Wayne's hand. He started to the driver's door. Then he looked back. "One more thing," Dan said.

Wayne waited.

"You want your old job back, you let me know," Dan said.

Wayne nodded. "I'll keep that in mind."

"You want it, it's there," Dan said. "It's got your name on it. Just say the word."

That afternoon, the heifer lay down. She stayed down that night and all the next day. Tuesday morning Wayne called back the veterinarian. He came within the hour.

"She eats?" the vet asked.

Wayne nodded yes.

"Bowel movements?" he asked, checking her temperature and looking into the gutter at the same time.

Wayne ran the fork through her manure, hoisted the tines.

The vet took the handle and pulled the fork closer for a look. A sniff. "That's cow dung in my book," he said. Then he turned to his leather case and took out a long stainless steel needle. He began to prick the needle along the heifer's spine; her skin shuddered at each touch. He moved the needle down her flank, her legs. He left a trail of red beads on the white hair.

The heifer scrabbled her legs once, and leaned away from the needle.

"That hurts? Good," the vet said. He straightened up and slowly wiped his needle. He stared down at the heifer, who turned to look at him. "No paralysis," he said. "She could get up if she wanted to. I've seen this before. In fact," the vet said, squinting with the effort of recall, "your dad had a heifer do this once. After five days or so she just stood up and that was that."

WAYNE'S HEIFER did not stand up that day or any day that week. She lay there, chewing her cud. She stared at the concrete wall. From inaction the hair on her hocks wore away to pink hide. The pink chafed to red meat that trickled blood, scabbed over, then broke open and bled again. Unused milk, heavy and yellow with colostrum, leaked from her udder and ran underneath her legs and belly, where it curdled to a sweet and sour smell. The milk drew flies. With a rope and an overhead pulley, Wayne daily rolled her from one side to the other. He washed her udder, her belly, the hot pits where her legs joined her body. Afterwards he dressed her hocks with salve. His invalid. His no-legged cow.

Nights Wayne dreamed. Once he threw on the barn lights to see her standing there, towering twice as tall as the other cows, the dead calf swinging behind, a tail with a head on it, a huge mouth snapping at flies, at anything that moved. He woke up sweating, his heart thudding in his ears.

Days, he came to believe that sometimes she stood up. That when he left the barn, she stood. He began to slip into the barn through the silo room or through the milk house door—but she was always lying down.

Unless of course she heard him coming. Cows could hear like deer and see like hawks, his father always said. Once, mid-day, Wayne drove the tractor around and around in the yard, gradually circling closer to the barn. Finally he parked beside it, left the engine running, climbed from its seat into the hay-loft, crept across the silent bales—then dropped through the haymow door. Lying there, she started.

The vet came again and gave her shots of vitamins. Anti-biotics.

When the vet had gone, Wayne swore at her, kicked her hard. She didn't turn to look.

THAT AFTERNOON he called down to Minneapolis, to Dan's house.

"Hello?" Ellen said.

"Hello," Wayne said.

She waited. She knew who it was.

"This is Wayne," he said.

"Okay," Ellen said.

"Let me talk to Judy," Wayne said.

"She's not in at the moment."

Wayne paused. He had not considered she wouldn't be in, that she wouldn't be there. "So where is she?"

"She's out."

Wayne was silent. "Where, out?"

"Out looking around."

"Looking around for what?" he said.

"Look—is there a message?" Ellen said.

Wayne paused. The phone wires hummed faraway. "The message is, there is no message."

ON THE TWELFTH evening, after supper, Wayne was lying on the couch when someone pounded on the door. Wayne jerked upright—he had not heard a car in the yard. He must have been sleeping.

In the dusk of the porch stood a short but sturdy man. He wore a dusty red cap whose brim, wicked full of scalp oil, was pulled low over his forehead. He had small eyes. A thin, dried trickle of Copenhagen lay in the right corner of his mouth. He was far older than Wayne first thought.

"Heard you've got one down," the man said.

"How's that?" Wayne said. He rubbed his face.

"You're Wayne Moen's boy?"

Wayne nodded.

"The one with the heifer down?"

Wayne nodded yes.

"Well then, let's get her up," the old man said.

"I KNEW your dad," the man said as they entered the barn. "He was a good cowman." He paused to look around. He stared at the hay in the manger, picked up a handful, held it to his nose. He looked into the gutter. At the ceiling. At the fork and broom hung straight, side by side, on the wall. Wayne was glad he had swept up.

"So where is she?" the old man said.

Wayne walked him to the heifer, who looked around once, then turned her face back to the wall.

The old man glanced up to the overhead pulley. "You been rolling her. Good." Then he produced a nail from his pocket, knelt, and drew it along her spine. The heifer's skin shivered, and the old man nodded and put away the nail.

He went around the front of the stanchions, to the heifer's head. Wayne followed. The man reached out to her long nose;

she shied. He murmured as he touched her. His fingers were short and brown and crooked on her white muzzle. He began to stroke the side of her head. At first she strained her neck away from him, then gradually she relaxed.

"Those vets work on the wrong end of a cow," the old man said softly. He continued to rub her muzzle in long, steady strokes. Slowly he moved his hand behind her ears, then down her throat. He murmured a hoarse, gravelly song to her. A baby-talk heifer song.

This went on.

"So," Wayne started to say.

"Shhhh!" the old man said.

Wayne leaned back against the wall and folded his arms.

As the lullaby went on, the heifer slowly began to move her head with the old man's stroking. Wayne watched. He checked his watch. Who the hell was this old man? As the heifer leaned deeper into his stroking, the old man eased his right arm around the heifer's neck. He moved his arm as slowly as water rising up the sides of a water tank, a slow creeping motion, too slow, almost, to see. At the same pace, he slid his left hand down the heifer's muzzle toward her nose. Wayne stared. Suddenly the old man clamped shut the heifer's jaws, jammed his fingers deep into her nostrils and screamed.

Wayne jerked backward, slammed one elbow against concrete. Sparks burned through his arm. He scrambled to keep from falling.

The old man danced, and screamed into the heifer's ear—he was a lunatic, a crazy man, a wild animal, a bobcat clamped over the heifer's mouth and nose. The heifer flailed her legs, bucked, scrambled, tried to jerk away from her attacker, tried to stand.

Tried to stand.

In that moment Wayne understood.

The heifer gained her feet. Nearly upright, her rear hooves pedaled, then at the last moment, slipped. She tipped sideways, then slammed back onto the concrete with a spray of straw dust and a hoot of air from her lungs. A milky spiderweb from her mouth blew across the alleyway and onto the concrete wall where it drooped, then began a slow crawl toward the straw.

The old man stood up. He wiped his fingers on his pants. "Close," he muttered, "and that trick only works once."

Wayne's heart pounded. He rubbed his elbow.

The old man stared at him briefly, then turned to the door. "Only one thing left to try."

Outside, Wayne heard the clank of steel. The old man returned carrying an iron device as tall as he was, an arm-thick shaft made of iron with two basketball-sized hoops bolted to it. The hoops slid on the shaft. Heavy setscrews tightened the hoops in place.

"Call it the Ironman," the old man said. "Made it myself. Pulled up a lot of cattle with the Ironman, here."

He went behind the heifer. The old man hooked Wayne's pulley onto a smaller center ring on the shaft, then laid the Ironman across the heifer's spine. "These hoops fit over the hip bones. You slide them up over the hip-pins until the hoops are good and tight, then you tighten the setscrews on the shaft. But you got to be careful," he said, snugging the hoops against the heifer's hide. "You set the hoops too tight, you pinch the hip nerves and then you're finished. You set them too loose, you get the heifer halfway up and she'll drop out. Then you break a leg." His voice softened as he worked. With a wrench he cranked tight the setscrews, then rocked the Ironman back and forth. The heifer, wearing the iron yoke, moved with him. She twisted to see what lay across her back. "She's ready—" the old man said.

Wayne and the man leaned into the pulley rope. The heifer's hips began to rise. She bellowed. She scrambled and gained her front legs.

"Faster—" the old man said.

They pulled.

The heifer bellowed louder and tried with her hind legs to scramble away from the Ironman.

"Higher," the old man said.

Her legs bicycled air. "Grab her legs, set them straight," the old man called. "We got to let her down."

Wayne planted the heifer's legs and the old man began to loosen the rope, to lower her. Wayne held her hooves wide and square on the straw. The old man let the rope go slack.

The heifer stood on her own.

The old man spun loose the setscrews and Wayne helped him lift away the Ironman.

The heifer turned to stare. She looked about her, then bellowed once, a long bleating note. She let herself tip to the side, then crashed back to the straw.

Wayne cursed.

The old man stared. Then he shrugged and turned to Wayne. "She can stand as good as you or me, she just doesn't want to. There's not much you can do about that 'cept drag her outside. Maybe there she'll forget."

"Forget what?" Wayne said.

"The why," the old man answered. "The why part." He hoisted the Ironman over his shoulder and turned to leave. "Get her outside, give her a couple of days. If she doesn't stand up you'll just have to get on with things."

THAT NIGHT he called for Judy again. Ellen answered.

"Let me talk to her," Wayne said.

"She's in bed," Ellen said.

"It's only nine o'clock," Wayne said.

"She's had a long day."

"Doing what?" he said.

"I told you," Ellen said, "she's been out. Looking around."

"Looking for work," Wayne said.

"I didn't say that," Ellen said.

"I said it," Wayne said. "Mark that down. I'm the one who said 'work.' "

There was silence.

"Is there a message?" Ellen said.

"To her or to you?" Wayne said.

The phone clicked dead in his ear.

THE NEXT DAY, with two young men from the feed mill, with ropes and the tractor, Wayne dragged the heifer from the barn into sunlight. She blinked and blinked her eyes against the new light. She made no sound. Wayne set out for her a pail of water, a pan of grain, and a half-bale of his best alfalfa, then went inside the barn and watched her through the window. She stared about the yard for a long time, turning once for a small mouthful of hay, then stared again.

Wayne watched her that evening from the house. He had only to look up from the TV and through the living room and there she was, a plump black-and-white throw rug in the yard. A cow's-head throw rug, the newest fashion in gracious farm living.

Much later that night Wayne awoke and went downstairs. He held aside the curtain and switched on the porch light. The little bulb lit up only the front of the yard; beyond the light, two green eyes shone bright and small, green eyes on a larger bulk, like some faraway ship, a tanker with two green running lights, far out to sea, unmoving, low, dead in the water. Wayne squinted and the heifer's white patches slowly came into focus, spills of white in the dark. Below the green eyes something swelled and shrank, swelled and shrank, something bobbing white and slow and regular in the blackness. It was her jaw. She was chewing and staring steadily into the light.

In the morning Wayne forked away her dung, filled her water pail. On his way to breakfast he fed her hay and grain, and in this way she became part of his regular chores. A half-shovel of grain, a flake of hay, a pail of water. He no longer imagined her standing. She was The Lying-down Heifer in the Yard.

On the third night Wayne awoke from a dream. A crawling dream. The blankets were twisted around his legs and he was breathing hard. He went downstairs and switched on the porch light. The two green eyes. The slow bobbing. "Saturday," he said to the empty living room. "Saturday is the last day."

On Friday, with ropes and 2 × 6 planking Wayne built a wooden-framed box with a sling inside, something like burn patients might lie in. With a tractor and loader he pushed the heifer sideways into the box and onto the ropes; then, with the loader, he slowly tilted the whole box upright. But the planks bent, then snapped, and the rope twisted around her neck—he had to leap down and cut her free before she choked to death. She flopped back to the ground with one short bellow, then lay there staring at him. Wayne swore. He snatched up a broken plank and beat her across the haunches until his hands stung, then grabbed a splinter of board and jabbed her flanks until blood came—then in mid-blow flung the wooden spear far across the yard.

In the house, panting, he fumbled through the phone book, tearing some of the pages until he found the number of Central Bi-Products, the dead animal service. He dialed. A woman answered. He gave directions. "Say," the woman said, "are you all right?"

That evening Wayne watered the heifer but gave her no hay or grain. Why the hell should he?

That night he dreamed. Another accident dream, a power-takeoff, a failing hydraulic, something large floating down onto him, onto his legs. He lay in the hospital on black sheets with white bandages on his stumps. When he returned, legless, to the farm he pulled himself about with a spiderwebbed system of pulleys and ropes. He awoke an hour before the alarm, his legs tingling.

At sunup on Saturday, Wayne carried his shotgun and a single slug to the barn. He leaned the gun in the corner of the pump room. The dead animal truck would not come until 10:00 A.M. She had until then. But Wayne was still milking at 7:45 A.M. when a truck rumbled into the yard, a tall dusty dump truck with a covered box and a logo on the side of a steer's head haloed by silhouettes of shoes and paint brushes and cans and jars of things. Wayne swore. He turned back to shut down his milkers. The truck driver, a thin man in brown-speckled coveralls and thick glasses, appeared in the doorway. "So where is it?" he called.

"Out front," Wayne replied, bleeding air from the milkers. "Give me a minute here."

"Out front is a live animal," the driver said.

Wayne stood up to stare.

"You see what it says on the side of the truck?" the driver said, peering at Wayne, then jerking his head behind him, through the doorway. "It says 'dead' animal service. You want live animal service, you call a vet."

Wayne stalked rapidly past the man and into the pump room, where he switched off the motor and came out with the shotgun. The driver's eyes widened and he stepped back. Wayne went to the heifer and shot her through the middle of her forehead; she jerked, stiffened her legs, then her head drooped and she began to bleed from her nose. "Dead? Now she's dead, okay?" Wayne shouted. He waved the shotgun at the driver.

The driver held up a hand and stepped backwards, closer to his truck. "Easy, easy does it—" he said. "Alls I meant was, I hate it when people do this because now she's going to bleed all over my truck—but that's not a problem," he added quickly. "I can hose down the whole floor in just a few minutes when I get back to the plant."

"Well good," Wayne said. His voice shook. His hands shook, too. The gun shook. "That's real good, mister, that's what I like to hear, some good news."

"Yessir, you're right about that," the driver said. "The good news is, we don't have no problem here."

Keeping his eyes on Wayne, the driver stepped backwards to the rear door of the truck and let it rattle up. Behind him, deep inside the trailer, dim in the light was a pile of animals, cows and goats and hogs all tumbled atop one another, bal-looned up, legs straight out, a pile of animal balloons or else

huge mushrooms growing from the damp wood. From beneath
the pile a single trickle of clear liquid wavered into view. It
followed the grain of planking, crawled across the bumper, and
began to drip onto the gravel.

The driver rattled out a steel ramp, then unreeled a heavy
chain. Keeping his eyes on Wayne, he slipped the chain under
the heifer's neck, then hooked it. He stepped back, then with
one lever brought up the RPMs of the truck's engine, and with
another lever engaged the spool. The spool began to wind back
the chain. The chain clattered on the ramp, then rose up to silence, tightening, swaying in the air like a power line drawn
up between its poles. On the ground the heifer's neck began to
stretch. In the instant before she began to slide, Wayne thought
her head would pull off. Then she jerked forward across the
gravel, moved smoothly up the ramp, and faster still across the
wet wood floor. Behind her the ramp glistened in the sunlight.
Flies dove toward its sheen.

"No problem at all, nossir," the driver said, shutting down
the levers. He kept glancing toward Wayne as he slid away
the ramp, then clattered down the rear door. He scribbled out
a receipt for Wayne, then hopped inside the cab. With a jerk
the truck accelerated away. In the rear the animals shifted. A
hoof thudded against the metal wall.

THAT EVENING Wayne took a bath. After chores he sat in
the tub in hot water for a long time. He washed his hair,
trimmed his fingernails and toenails. Afterwards he put on a
clean shirt and pants, then went out to eat. He drove to Margie's Wagon Wheel, a supper club north of town. Its orange
wagon wheel winked along the highway, and Wayne turned
his pickup into the lot. There were plenty of cars already
parked. A sharp drumroll and the thud of a bass guitar came
from inside. A band warming up. It was already nine o'clock,
and Wayne hurried forward.

At the door he glanced up at the neon wagon wheel, then
paused for a closer look. Its orange spokes blinked in sequence

and made the wheel turn, or at least seem to turn. But it was the black electrical tape, wound around the glass tubing, that divided the orange into spokes and hubs, that formed letters, that dotted the *i*'s. Just black tape. He wondered why he had never thought of that before.

Inside Margie's Wagon Wheel were knotty pine tables and booths to the left, a horseshoe-shaped bar at center, the band and dance floor to the right. A haze of cigarette smoke and fried chicken smell hung just below the ceiling. Waitresses in white blouses and red aprons moved among the booths and among the tables, and the jukebox bumped some song against the warm-up riffs from the band.

"One?" a waitress said to Wayne.

"Just me," Wayne said. He smiled at her but she had already turned away. He followed her.

He ordered a broasted chicket basket, coleslaw, and fries. The fries were salty and he drank three bottles of Bud during the meal. He ate and watched the people. Tourists in shorts and knit shirts. Young waitresses with curly blond hair and faces tanned past brown to red, which meant they'd spent all day at the lakes. At the bar were a few locals wearing seed-caps and shirts with the sleeves cut off at the shoulders; they sipped beer and watched the young waitresses come and go. Wayne remembered some of the bar drinkers from high school. They were a grade, several grades ahead of him. He didn't really know them.

Finished with the chicken, Wayne tore open the little packet with the alcohol napkin and wiped his mouth and fingers. By now the band was playing louder and people danced. His waitress took away the basket of chicken bones and the ketchup, wiped his table. "Will that do it tonight?" she said. She smiled brightly, and for the first time, stood still. She was close enough to Wayne for him to smell coconut oil beneath her clothes.

"One chicken, down the hatch," Wayne said.

She waited, still smiling. Behind her, at the front, two or three couples waited for booths.

"Sure, that'll do it," Wayne said.

She wrote out his ticket, put a smiling face and a "Thanx, Terri!" on the back.

He had a ten and some ones, but at the last moment paid her with a twenty.

She brought his change back to the booth.

"There you go," she said.

"And there you go," Wayne said.

"Thanks!" she said, surprised. "You have yourself a good night now, all right?"

"I always do," Wayne said. He grinned up at her, but she had already turned away to the front, to a couple waiting for his booth.

Wayne took a seat at the far end of the bar, and ordered a tequila with a Bud chaser. He watched the dancers and burped chicken. The band played loud Credence Clearwater and thumping Merle Haggard. He liked the music, the good-smelling cigarette smoke, the colored lights. He wondered why he had not come here before.

He was sipping his third tequila when a woman's voice behind him said loudly, "Hey there, Wayney Moen!" Wayne saw her in the bar mirror before he turned. A round pie of a face, blue circles of eye makeup, upswept blond hair.

Wayne turned.

"That face," he said, "I know that face." Behind her was a tanned older man.

"Christ, I'm not that fat." The woman giggled.

"You're not fat," the man behind her said without turning. He was middle-aged, wore white shoes, burgundy pants, and a white belt over which the small pod of a belly hung. His eyes followed Wayne's waitress. Terri.

"Come on, Wayney Moen, think—" the blond woman commanded. "Study hall. Mr. Sherp's history class. Old Man Weeder's English class."

"Beverly Hoffman," Wayne said. He smiled and put out his hand. Hers was fat and moist.

"Shirley Hoffman," she said. "Shirley Hoffman Anderson Karjula Hoffman, to be exact."

"I'll be damned," Wayne said.

"Me too, I think," she said with a conspiratorial whisper. Then she laughed loudly.

Wayne kept smiling.

"A joke," she said. "Like all my names. Jokes. No, not jokes, jokers." She giggled. "Anyway, this year I finally take my real name back, and now he comes along and wants to change it," she said. She giggled again. "To Petermeyer."

Wayne nodded to the man behind.

"That's right," the man said. He grinned briefly at Wayne, then let his eyes turn back to Terri.

"What kind of name is Petermeyer?" Shirley said to Wayne.

"Petermeyer?" Wayne said. He shrugged. He was remembering her from high school now, a thin blond girl with round eyes and slightly buck teeth.

"Mister, I asked you a question," Shirley said. She leaned toward Wayne and narrowed her eyes, and put one hand on his shoulder to steady herself.

"Petermeyer," Wayne repeated.

"Sounds like Oscar Meyer, doesn't it?" she said, turning to the man. "Oscar Meyer and his weeny." She tipped backwards and hooted with laughter.

"Hey, easy does it," Petermeyer said to her. "You better sit down.

"On your weenie, I suppose?" she said. "Oscar?" She laughed again and stumbled against Petermeyer, nearly knocking him over. Wayne jumped forward and steadied them. He helped Petermeyer get her to a table.

"Thanks, buddy," Petermeyer said to Wayne.

"No problem," Wayne said. He turned away.

"Hey—pull up a chair," Petermeyer said. "Don't be a stranger."

SHIRLEY DOZED with her forehead on one wrist while Wayne and Petermeyer drank tequilas. "Shooters," Petermeyer called them. He kept holding up two fingers to the waitress.

Wayne lost count. His arms went numb.

Petermeyer talked about his job. He was in paper products, disposable towels mostly. Covered three states. "But condoms," he said, "now there's a growth industry."

Wayne and Petermeyer laughed loudly.

Shirley sat up abruptly—there was a red spot on her forehead—and turned to Wayne. "So how's about a dance, Wayney Moen?" she said.

"I don't know," Wayne said. He heard his words slur. "These shooters."

"Go on, go on," Petermeyer said. "You young folks have fun."

"Don't be a shit," Shirley said to Wayne, pulling him by the arm.

The band was playing "Green River," and Wayne fell into the beat. Shirley swayed in front of him. Her big tits bounced inside her silk blouse but her ankles and calves were trim, and she moved easily.

"You married?" she called to Wayne.

"Not sure," Wayne said.

Shirley laughed hysterically. "I get it, I'm with you!" She said.

Someone collided with Wayne and fell to the floor. Wayne picked the man up and they all continued dancing. The band swung into a faster song and Wayne and Shirley remained on the dance floor. Wayne began to swing his arms, do some dips. He had always considered himself a good dancer.

"That's it," Shirley called to him. "Now you're talking."

From the milking, the everyday bending, Wayne's legs were as limber as a ballet dancer's legs, and once he dropped to the floor in most of a split and bounced up again without missing a beat.

"Dance Fever!" Shirley shouted.

When the band broke, Wayne and Shirley stumbled back to the table. Petermeyer clapped for them. "Here, wet your whistles," he said. He pushed two shooters toward Wayne and Shirley.

"Jesus," Wayne panted.

"Double Jesus," Shirley said. "To your health—no, to marriage."

Wayne saluted them and threw down the shooter.

"He's not sure he's married," Shirley explained.

"I been there," Petermeyer said. "I'm with you on that one."

The tequila hit Wayne hard somewhere behind his eyes.

"He's not sure he's married," Shirley said to the next table and jerked her head at Wayne.

Wayne waved to them.

He turned back to Shirley. "But I could find out," he said.

"Find out?" Shirley said.

"If I'm married."

"How?"

"Call her," Wayne said. "I'll call and find out for sure."

"Right now?" Shirley said.

"Right now. Why not?" Wayne said. He was speaking loudly, could not control his volume, his lips.

"Rich!" Shirley shouted. "That's so rich!" Shirley stood up and pulled Wayne to his feet. "Ladies and gents—" she shouted. Faces turned.

"Get this, ladies and gents—this gentleman is not sure he's married, but he's going to call to find out for sure. Right now! He's going to call right now!"

Several people clapped.

Shirley pulled Wayne to the phone by the bar. She held out the receiver. He took it.

"Let's have a little goddamn quiet in here," she called to the bar.

More people turned. The noise fell.

"That's more like it," she said, and rattled in the quarter.

Wayne dialed. He waited a few moments, then looked back to Shirley. "She wants money."

"Your wife wants money? Already?"

"No, the phone operator."

People laughed. They dug in their pockets and coins flashed in the air, silver raining down on Wayne. One coin hit him hard on the forehead. Shirley went to her hands and knees and began to pick up quarters from the floor. When she had a handful she gave them to Wayne, and he poured them into the slot. Some spilled back onto the floor. Finally the phone began to ring on the other end.

As he waited, the tequila came and went like waves.

"Hello?" Ellen's voice said. She sounded groggy.

"Hey, hey," Wayne said, "this is the Big Bopper speaking!"

"Who is this?" Ellen said.

"It's Wayne," he said. He turned to Shirley. Shirley nodded enthusiastically and circled a finger for him to keep talking. "Wayney Moen," he said.

"It's after midnight," Ellen said. "Why are you calling this time of night?"

"Hey, loosen up," Wayne said.

"You're drunk," she said.

"Drinking yes, drunk, no. I wouldn't say drunk," Wayne said.

"I'm going to hang up," Ellen said.

"Wait—let me talk to her, I got a question," Wayne said.

"It's too late, you're drunk, you're not talking to her to-night."

"You know so much, I'll ask you," Wayne said. "Just one question, okay?"

There was silence on the line.

Around Wayne, people leaned in to listen.

"Am I still married?" Wayne said.

There was silence. Then Ellen said, "She got a job today. Where I work. I got her in. She's through with you."

"You bitch," Wayne began. "You lousy stinking—"

The phone clicked dead but he went on. He swore at her, words he never used, words he did not remember knowing, vicious words. Then he ran out of breath. He looked around. A ring of people holding drinks stared at him. He turned back to the phone. "So go to hell—we're through!" he said, and slammed down the receiver.

The crowd clapped.

Wayne bowed low.

There was a louder round of clapping and cheering, and back at the table with Petermeyer and Shirley, drinks came from all sides.

He awoke with an orange wheel of light in his face. To both sides was metal. He lay on metal. There was sky above. He blinked and sat up. The supper club. It was gray and silent, the parking lot empty but for his pickup and a rusted Cadillac. He had slept in the bed of his pickup and the orange wheel of light was the sun.

His heart picked up rhythm. The cows. The milking.

He checked his watch. Already six o'clock.

Wayne stumbled into the driver's seat, found the keys, started the engine. He pulled slowly onto the highway, closing one eye to keep the truck steady on the center line. He rolled down a window, and after a mile or two the cool air began to clear his head.

He squinted into the mirror. There was a cut on his forehead, a thin line of dried blood. His lips and eyelids were puffy with mosquito bites, and he made a face to see if everything still worked. "Jesus," he muttered, turning back to the road.

He thought about last night. He remembered the clapping, the cheering.

And the phone call.

Sure, he remembered the call. He remembered everything he said. He was drunk, yes, but he had gotten a lot of things off his chest. For drunk talk was straight talk. "What a man says drunk has been thought out beforehand." He'd read that somewhere.

He squinted at himself in the mirror. "Jesus," he said, and could not help but grin. It had been a night to remember.

Around him the sun shone on the fields. Its light lay flat and orange and lit up the crowns of the fields, and left dark eyes in the low places.

He turned onto gravel, to the reassuring snarl of small stones in the wheel wells. The road home. He drove and let the clear air and its dewy smell roll over him, no goddamn smell of burnt plastic on this road. He drove fast and felt light as a feather.

Which puzzled him.

His marriage was over but he felt good. Never better. He sped down the road, leaving a shining plume of dust behind. When the top of the silo and the barns came in sight, he honked the horn. What for? He didn't know. For the hell of it. As he turned the truck sharply into the yard he honked the horn again, long and loud this time. There was nobody to wake up.

Which was part of it, he realized.

He was home and there was nobody to wake up.

He parked by the garage and headed in the footpath toward the barn. Walking quickly on feet sore from dancing, Wayne was halfway to the barn when he halted. He looked around. Surrounding him, the buildings stood sunlit and neutral. He looked down to his boots.

The path.

He was squarely in the path yet he felt none of that lightness, no numb vertigo of legs and feet not his own. Felt, in short, none of his father. He threw back his head and laughed.

Just ahead of Wayne was the faint depression where the heifer had lain, the brown stain of her blood. He kicked one small stone toward the spot where she had lain. He felt nothing for her, no anger, no blame—because she too, like his father, was receding quickly into the past, herded along by some larger idea, some completely new thought rolling rapidly and with great force into the present.

Wayne waited. The idea gathered around him in the same way the sunlight was just now striking into the yard, lighting up the big open faces of the buildings.

He realized he was alone.

In the house, in the barns and granaries, in the fields, there was no one here, no one home.

His father was gone.

His mother was gone.

His wife was gone.

The heifer was gone.

All of them were gone and they would not come back. No one lived here now but himself. He was finally home and he would never have to go anywhere again.

THE UNDECLARED MAJOR

IN HIS GLOOMY periods Walter Hansen saw himself as one large contradiction. He was still twenty, yet his reddish hair was in full retreat from the white plain of his forehead. He had small and quick-moving blue eyes, eyes that tended skyward, eyes that noted every airplane that passed overhead; his hands and feet were great, heavy shovels. As Walter shambled between his classes at the University of Minnesota in Minneapolis, he sometimes caught unexpected sight of himself in a tall glass doorway or window. He always stopped to stare: there he was, the big farm kid with a small handful of books. Walter Hansen, the only twenty-year-old Undeclared Major on the whole campus.

But even that wasn't true. Walter Hansen had declared a major some time ago; he just hadn't felt up to telling anyone what it was.

At present Walter sat in the last, backward-facing seat of the Greyhound bus, reading *The Collected Stories of John Cheever*. Occasionally he looked up to stare at the blue-tinted fields, which in their passing pulled him, mile by mile, toward home. Toward his twenty-first birthday this very weekend.

By the third hour of the trip Walter had a headache from reading. He put away Cheever and began to watch the passing farms. It was a sunny, wet April in central Minnesota. Farmers were trying to spread manure. Their tractors left black

ruts in the yellow corn stubble, and once Walter saw two tractors chained together straining, the big rear wheels spinning,
throwing clods in the air, as they tried to pull free a third
spreader sunk to its hubs beneath an overenthusiastic load of
dung.

At the end of the fourth hour Walter's hometown came
onto the horizon. It was low and scattered, and soon began to
flash by in the windows of the slowing bus like a family slide
show that was putting to sleep even the projector operator.
A junkyard with a line of shining hubcaps nailed on the fence.
A combination deer farm and aquarium with its stuffed black
bear wearing a yellow hula skirt, and wheels that stood by the
front door. Then the tall and narrow white wooden houses.
The square red brick buildings of Main Street, where the bus
sighed to a stop at the Shell station. Ducking his head, Walter
clambered down the bus steps and stood squinting in the sunlight.

Main Street was three blocks long. Its two-story buildings
were fronted with painted tin awnings or cedar shake shingles
to disguise the brick and make the buildings look lower and
more modern. At the end of Main Street was the taller, dull
gray tower of the feed mill. A yellow drift of cornmeal lay
on its roof. A blue wheel of pigeons turned overhead. At the
stoplight a '57 Chevy chirped its tires, accelerated rapidly for
half a block, then braked sharply to turn down Main Street.

Which Walter planned to avoid. On Main Street he would
have to speak to people. They would ask him things.

"Walt—so how's the rat race?"

"Walt—where does a person park down there?"

"So Walt, what was it you're going into again? Business?
Engineering? Vetinary?"

Carrying his small suitcase, and looking neither left nor
right, Walter slipped undetected across Main Street. He walked
two blocks to the railroad crossing where he set out east.

The iron rails shone blue. Between the rails, tiny agates
glinted red from their bed of gravel, and the flat, sun-warmed
railroad ties exhaled a faint breath of creosote. On Walter's

right, a robin dug for worms on the sunny south embankment; on the north side, the dirty remnant of a snowbank leaked water downhill. Walter stopped to poke at the snowbank with a stick. Beneath a black crust and mud and leaves, the snow was freshly white and sparkling—but destined, of course, to join the muddy pond water below. Walter thought about that. About destiny. He stood with the chill on his face from the old snowbank and the sun warm on his neck and back. There was a poem buried somewhere in that snowbank. Walter waited, but the first line would not visit him. He walked on.

Walter was soon out of town and into woods and fields. Arms outstretched, suitcase balanced atop his head, he walked one rail for twenty-two ties, certainly a record of some sort. Crows called. A red-headed woodpecker flopped from east to west across the rails. The bird was ridiculously heavy for the length of its wings, a fact which made Walter think of Natural Science. Biology. Veterinary Medicine and other majors with names as solid and normal as fork handles.

Animal Husbandry.

Technical Illustration.

Mechanical Engineering.

Ahead on Walter's left was a twenty-acre field of new oat seeding, brown in the low spots, dusty chartreuse on the higher crowns of the field.

Plant Science.

He could tell people he was developing new wheat strains for Third World countries, like Norman Borlaug.

He walked on, slower now, for around a slight bend he could see, a half mile ahead, the gray dome of his father's silo and the red shine of the dairy barn. He neared the corner post of the west field, where his father's land began. Half the field was gray, the other half was freshly black. He slowed further. A meadowlark called from a fence post. Walter stopped to pitch a rock at the bird.

Then he heard a tractor. From behind a broad swell in the field rose his father's blue cap, tan face, brown shirt, then the red snout of the Massey-Ferguson. The Massey pulled their green four-row corn planter. His father stood upright on the platform of the tractor. He stood that way to sight down the tractor's nose, to keep its front tires on the line scuffed in the dirt by the corn planter's marker on the previous round. Intermittently Walter's father swiveled his neck for a glance back at the planter. He looked, Walter knew, for the flap of a white rag tied around the main shaft; if the white flag waved, the main shaft turned, the planter plates revolved, pink kernels fell—Walter knew all that stuff.

He stopped walking. There were bushes along the fence-row, and he stooped to lower his profile, certain that his father hadn't seen him. First Walter wanted to go home, talk to his mother, have a cup of coffee. Two cups, maybe. A cinnamon roll. A bowl of bing cherries in sauce, with cream. Maybe one more splash of coffee. Then. Then he'd come back to the field to speak with his father.

Nearing the field's end, his father trailed back his right arm, found the cord, which he pulled at the same moment as he turned hard to left. Brakes croaked. Tripped, the marker arms rose, the Massey came hard around with its front wheels reaching for their new track, the planter straightened behind, the right arm with its shining disk fell, and his father, back to Walter, headed downfield.

Except that brakes croaked again and the tractor came to a stop. His father turned to Walter and held up a hand.

Walter waved once. He looked briefly behind him to the rails that led back toward town, then crossed the ditch and swung his suitcase over the barbed wire.

His father shut off the tractor. "Hey, Walt—" his father called.

Walter waved again.

His father waited by the corn planter. He smiled, his teeth white against the tan skin, the dust. Walter came up to him.

"Walt," his father said.

They stood there grinning at each other. They didn't shake hands. Growing up, Walter believed people shook hands only in the movies or on used-car lots. None of his relatives ever shook hands. Their greeting was to stand and grin at each other and raise their eyebrows up and down. At the university Walter and his circle of friends shook hands coming and going, European style.

"How's it going?" Walter said, touching his boot to the corn planter.

"She's rolling," his father said. "Got one disk that keeps dragging, but other than that."

People in Walter's family often did not complete their sentences.

"A disk dragging," Walter said.

"Yep," his father said. He squinted at Walter, looked down at his clean clothes. "What would you do for a stuck disk?" he asked.

"I'd take out the grease zerk and run a piece of wire in there. That failing, I'd take off the whole disk and soak it in a pan of diesel fuel overnight," Walter said.

Father and son grinned at each other.

His father took off his hat. His forehead was white, his hair coppery.

"So how's the rat race, son?"

"Not so bad," Walter said.

His father paused a moment. "Any . . . decisions yet?" his father said.

Walter swallowed. He looked off toward town. "About . . . a major, you mean?" Walter said.

His father waited.

"Well," Walter said. His mouth went dry. He swallowed twice. "Well," he said, "I think I'm going to major in English."

His father pursed his lips. He pulled off his work gloves one finger at a time. "English," he said.

"English," Walter nodded.

His father squinted. "Son, we already know English."

Walter stared. "Well, yessir, that's true. I mean, I'm going to study literature. Books. See how they're written. Maybe write one of my own some day."

His father rubbed his brown neck and stared downfield.

Two white sea gulls floated low over the fresh planting.

"So what do you think?" Walter said.

His father's forehead wrinkled and he turned back to Walter. "What could a person be, I mean with that kind of major? An English major," his father said, testing the phrase on his tongue and his lips.

"Be," Walter said. He fell silent. "Well, I don't know, I could be a . . . writer. A teacher maybe, though I don't think I want to teach. At least not for a while. I could be . . ." Then Walter's mind went blank. As blank and empty as the fields around him.

His father was silent. The meadowlark called again.

"I would just be myself, I guess," Walter said.

His father stared a moment at Walter. "Yourself, only smarter," he added.

"Yessir," Walter said quickly, "that's it."

His father squinted downfield at the gulls, then back at Walter. "Nobody talked you into this?"

Walter shook his head no.

"You like it when you're doing it?" his father asked. He glanced across his own field, at what he had planted.

Walter nodded.

His father looked back to Walter and thought another moment. "You think you can make a living at it?"

"Somehow," Walter said.

His father shrugged. "Then I can't see any trouble with it myself," he said. He glanced away, across the fields to the next closest set of barns and silos. "Your uncles, your grampa, they're another story, I suppose."

"They wouldn't have to know," Walter said quickly.

His father looked back to Walter and narrowed his eyes. "They ask me, I'll tell them," he said.

Walter smiled at his father. He started to take a step closer, but at that moment his father looked up at the sun. "We better keep rolling here," he said. He tossed his gloves to Walter. "Take her around once or twice while I eat my sandwich."

Walter climbed onto the tractor and brought up the RPMs.
In another minute he was headed downfield. He stood upright
on the platform and held tightly to the wheel. The leather
gloves were still warm and damp from his father's hands. He
sighted the Massey's radiator cap on the thin line in the dirt
ahead, and held it there. Halfway downfield he remembered
to check the planter flag; in one backward glance he saw his
father in straight brown silhouette against the chartreuse band
of the fencerow bushes, saw the stripe of fresh dirt unrolling
behind, the green seed canisters, and below, the white flag waving. He let out a breath.

After two rounds, Walter began to relax. He began to feel
the warm thermals from the engine, the cool breath of the
earth below. Gulls hovered close over the tractor, their heads
cocked earthward as they waited for the disks to turn up yellow cutworms. A red agate passed underneath and was covered
by dirt. The corn planter rolled behind, and through the trip
rope, a cotton cord gone smoothly black from grease and dusty
gloves, Walter felt the shafts turning, the disks wheeling, the
kernels dropping, the press wheel tamping the seed into four
perfect rows.

Well, not entirely perfect rows.

Walter, by round four, had begun to think of other things.
That whiteness beneath the old snowbank. The blue shine of
the iron rails. The damp warmth of father's gloves. The heavy,
chocolate-layer birthday cake that he knew, as certain as he
knew the sun would set tonight and rise tomorrow, his mother
had hidden in the pantry. Of being twenty-one and the limit-
less destiny, the endless prospects before him, Walter Hansen,
English Major.

As he thought about these and other things, the tractor and
its planter drifted a foot to the right, then a foot to the left,
centered itself, then drifted again. At field's end his father stood
up. He began to wave at Walter first with one hand, then both.
But Walter drove on, downfield, smiling slightly to himself,
puzzling over why it was he so seldom came home.

YOU ARE WHAT YOU DRIVE

ONE BRIGHT winter morning in February of 1969, in the Deerlake, Minnesota, Chevrolet/GMC/Ford/Chrysler/Buick Dealership where the tall windows were reduced to portholes by brilliant white frost, Mrs. Fulton G. Anderson drew one finger across the roof of the new Buick LeSabre. Its paint was black and smooth. Sunlight bloomed golden in the chromed mirror. From below, she could smell the leather of its seats, the fresh rubber of its tires.

Mrs. Anderson swallowed. Her husband, the Reverend Anderson, had died suddenly the previous year, in December; his life insurance money was sitting in the bank. The Anderson's present car, a Ford, was on its second hundred thousand miles. In winter, ankle-biting drafts leaked through the floorboards; in summer, dust. Mrs. Anderson's only child, Beth, a thin, studious girl with a long neck, was already a senior at Luther College in Decorah, Iowa, and had good prospects for teaching high school English (though no prospects whatsoever for a husband unless she began to take more pride in her appearance; but unwashed hair, floppy hats, purple sweatshirts, and long black skirts would pass, Mrs. Anderson believed, because children went through phases). Right now Mrs. Anderson wished Beth were here. They had always included Beth in family decisions.

"Go ahead," the auto salesman said. He was a young fellow, Beth's age, with big teeth and tiny dried razor nicks on his Adam's apple. "Put yourself behind the wheel," he said with a grin.

Mrs. Anderson drew back her finger, kicked a tire.

THAT AFTERNOON Mrs. Anderson wrote Beth.

Her daughter's letter came by return post. Beth wrote that the Buick seemed like a lot of money for just a car. She said that a luxury car like the LeSabre was, considering the division of wealth in the world, one of the most repugnant of American metaphors. She wrote that, rather than buying the Buick, Mrs. Anderson ought to donate the insurance money to the Mary Knoll nuns laboring in Central America, then use public transportation to get around Deerlake.

After Mrs. Anderson read Beth's letter she looked out the kitchen window to the bird feeder. Several chickadees pecked at cracked corn. She watched the little birds without really seeing them, just their brief gray flutters, their minor comings and goings in the periphery of her mind, and waited to be visited by her true opinion of Beth's letter. Suddenly a single fluffed-up chickadee, a big fellow, lit squarely in the yellow corn and stared straight at her through the glass. Mrs. Anderson blinked. She squinted and leaned closer to the window. How truly gray his grays, how sharply drawn his blacks and whites!

She found a pen and wrote Beth a brief note reminding her there was no public transportation in Deerlake, never had been.

The pastor at First Lutheran encouraged Mrs. Anderson to buy the Buick. First, he said, the way the Indians drove—especially during the autumn ricing season—one needed a safe car, and it was the big front-engine American cars like the LeSabre that always came out best in head-on collisions. Second, he said, she was already sixty-three. The Buick would be the last car she'd ever have to buy.

That night Mrs. Anderson sat bolt upright from a deep

sleep: in her own room she had heard someone say, loudly, "Yes!"

IN NINE years Mrs. Anderson drove the LeSabre 18,142 miles. During this time Beth went on to graduate school in English, first for an M.A. at Iowa City and then for the Ph.D. at Purdue. Beth returned home to Deerlake regularly at Christmas and Easter, always alone, and talked endlessly about a French novelist called Alain-Fournier who had died tragically—heroically, actually—at age twenty-eight. Fournier was perhaps the first man killed in World War I. Beth had written her dissertation on Fournier, and now was enlarging the dissertation into a book because she had decided she wanted to be an essayist or a novelist; publishing the Fournier book, even with a small house, might be her big break. Summers, Beth traveled by train or Greyhound bus back and forth across the country to college writers' conferences. There she stayed in low redbrick dormitories for two weeks at a time and got tips from famous writers during wine and cheese hours.

Each Christmas and Easter Mrs. Anderson listened to Beth talk on of Fournier and of other things one could write about. A hot topic the year before had been depression, Beth said, but she hadn't realized it until depression had peaked and the magazines had gone on to breast cancer. After a few years of this, whenever Beth began to talk of Fournier or of writing, Mrs. Anderson's mind automatically shifted into reverse, to Beth back in high school, Beth winning at debates and at spelling bees. However, by Easter of 1978, when Mrs. Anderson was seventy-two, she thought mainly about who it was who was to take her grocery shopping. In the previous year, the year of depression, Mrs. Anderson had begun to drive the LeSabre an inch too close to things.

To the drive-in window at the bank.

To the pumps at the gas station.

To both sides of her own garage.

People from church, especially those with small children who rode bicycles around town, now drove Mrs. Anderson about Deerlake. Any time, anywhere, they told her, just call.

Of course Mrs. Anderson didn't need to call when Beth was home. Beth drove her mother about in the Buick. Beth drove and complained about a funny ticking noise somewhere in the car. Try as she might, Mrs. Anderson could not hear the noise.

"That fellow Sylvester Harjula," Mrs. Anderson said. She was surprised to have remembered his full name. "The dark-haired fellow you went to high school with. He has a mustache now. Maybe I should have him look into it—they say he can fix anything." Mrs. Anderson looked over at Beth. At her daughter's long neck, her thin blond hair that needed a good washing and then a body perm. "He's not a bad-looking man either," she added.

"Really, Mother!" Beth said. Her neck colored pink.

When Mrs. Anderson turned seventy-five she happened onto a *Reader's Digest* article, "The Cruel Cost of Aging." The next day, without writing Beth, Mrs. Anderson dusted off the windshield of the LeSabre and drove it carefully back to the dealership. There she learned firsthand a lesson about depreciation—how when a person puts the key into the ignition of a new car, one thousand dollars flies out the window. (She imagined green dollar bills streaming out the window and fluttering down the road behind.) She also learned that people preferred smaller Japanese and German cars these days.

Mrs. Anderson took the check for the LeSabre and walked three blocks to the bank's drive-in window. There she placed the check in the little tin tube and pushed the button. With a hiss her check disappeared down the pipe—which suddenly reminded her of another *Readers' Digest* article: the similarities between rural banks of today and rural banks of the 1930s.

She spoke into the microphone, then waited. Her heart pounded. After a long while the pipe hissed and the little tube popped into daylight. Mrs. Anderson retrieved, in cash, one half of the LeSabre money. At home she placed the money in a one-pound coffee can which she then stored in the freezer beneath several square packages of frozen corn dated 1969.

AT THE dealership the LeSabre was scheduled for the body shop. It needed front and rear bumpers. New chrome door guards. Rocker panels. Quarter panels. Paint. That same morning Big Ed Hawkinson was driving his Kenworth logging truck past the car lot when from the corner of his eye he spied something different. Something black. He set the air brakes and skidded his rig to a stop. Big Ed was a logger, a Christmas tree farmer, and an auto body man during the coldest months of the winter. Every fall during ricing season he made a few bucks selling junkers to the Indians. At the moment, however, Big Ed was looking for a better-than-average unit, something a notch or two up. His oldest boy, Elvis, was getting his driver's license this very week. Big Ed never knew exactly what he was looking for in a car until he saw it, and what Big Ed was seeing, there next in line at the body-shop door, was the old Anderson widow's LeSabre.

ELVIS HAWKINSON drove the LeSabre home and straight into Big Ed's body shop. Elvis had plans for the LeSabre. He saw it painted metal flake blue, saw it with rear leaf-spring risers and Cragar mags, saw inside red shag carpet on the dash and a Jensen stereo system that would tear your scalp off. But there was one problem. The LaSabre was a four-door. Four-door cars were for women hauling around curtain climbers and bags of diapers and Kotex.

Elvis worked thirty hours straight. He knocked off the rear door handles and fiberglassed the holes. He welded the rear doors shut, then sanded smooth the welding bead. With a toilet plunger he popped out the rear quarter panels. He stripped all the chrome, glassed the screw holes, sanded everything again, then taped the windshield and all the glass. Toward morning of the second day, he shot the whole car with rust-colored primer.

After breakfast Elvis led Big Ed and Jimmy out to the shop.

"So what do you think?" Elvis said happily. He held a screwdriver and was about to open the gallon of blue metal flake.

"Well . . ." Big Ed said. He ran his hand through his hair.
"You ask me, it looks like a sixty-nine four-door LeSabre with
the back doors welded shut and then primed," Jimmy said.

Elvis looked at the LeSabre. At Big Ed. At the can of blue
metal flake.

That fall Elvis drove the LeSabre, still primed, with no Cragar mags and no Jensen stereo, back and forth to International
Falls Community College where he took classes in diesel me-
chanics and hydraulics. The drive was 125 miles one way. At the
end of two years the LeSabre had 62,879 miles on it and Elvis
Hawkinson had enlisted in the Air Force.

JIMMY HAWKINSON, Elvis's younger brother, put chrome
wheels on the rear of the LeSabre and added twelve-inch risers
to the rear leaf springs. The risers caused two problems. First,
the rear bumper now stood forty-two inches off the ground,
and Jimmy, who was five feet five, or only sixty-five inches
tall, could not jump high enough to reach into the trunk.
Second, the rear risers also threw the headlight beams directly
onto the highway, like two floor lamps. But these were not
large problems. Jimmy built a small wooden step stool which
he carried on the back seat, in case he needed to get into the
trunk; and when driving at night he simply left the headlight
beams on bright.

Jimmy further customized the LeSabre. He tore out the
front bench-type seat and welded in its place two bucket seats
he had gotten from a wrecked Datsun 280Z. To the dashboard
he added an eight-track stereo. He was saving for a gallon of
red metal flake, but his car payment made things tough.

Every week Jimmy sent thirty dollars to Ensign Elvis Hawkinson, Third Diesel Support Squadron, c/o Fourth Tactical
Squadron, Fifth Fleet, Pensacola, Florida. He sent the thirty
dollars for two weeks. He missed the third week because he
had bought the chrome wheels. He made the next week's payment, but could muster only twenty dollars the following
week. Missed the next week. Missed the week after that. At

the end of three months he stopped sending anything, though he did write to Elvis asking what exactly were the dates when Elvis would be home on leave.

Elvis showed up for Christmas two days earlier than planned, but Jimmy and the LeSabre had left the day before. A business trip. Jimmy left a note for Elvis and for Big Ed, saying that he was heading out to work in the gas fields in Wyoming. A week later he wrote again, a card postmarked Buffalo. He didn't say what outfit he was working for. He did write that there was so much natural gas in Wyoming it came up in water pipes; that you could turn on a faucet, light a match, and have fire and water coming from the same tap.

In March, Jimmy wrote Big Ed that Wyoming was deader than road kill and he was heading down to Texas, to the oil fields. He said that's where the work was.

In May, Jimmy Hawkinson hitchhiked into Deerlake from the south. He found Big Ed working on the Kenworth boom, hunkered over the bright spark of the welder. When Big Ed finally tipped back his mask and saw Jimmy, he stood up. Father and son grinned at each other. They shook hands. Jimmy didn't remember ever shaking hands with Big Ed. In a rush of words, Jimmy told Big Ed that he was ready now to work with him in the body shop or in the woods or trimming Christmas trees, wherever he was needed. Jimmy felt dumbshit happy and more than a little like crying. He told Big Ed that he'd always wanted to work at home with his own father, but for some reason he had to get way far away before he saw it. And one more thing: Could he borrow the Kenworth to drive down to Minneapolis to pick up the LeSabre?

SYLVESTER HARJULA, a bachelor with deeply bitten fingernails, was the sole proprietor of a one-banner used-car lot at the Deerlake city limits. He bought the old Anderson LeSabre off the Hawkinson truck for ten tens cash. He would have paid more—a lot more, for here was the car Beth Anderson herself had driven. Here was the car that finally would give Syl-

vester a real excuse to talk to Beth Anderson when she came
home for Christmas. But a hundred bucks was a hundred
bucks.

The LeSabre was cold iron stew. The engine had thrown a
rod through the block and clear into the battery. The trunk
lid was gone. The left rear door was punched in with the outline of a parking meter. The transmission bled red through its
seals like a lung-shot deer, and the odometer was a dead clock
stopped at 17,847 miles. Yet none of this necessarily bothered
Sylvester. With cars, where other people saw rust, Sylvester
saw Bondo. Where other people saw blue oil smoke in the
exhaust and turned away, Sylvester saw piston rings and maybe
sleeves. SYLVESTER HARJULA'S NO PROBLEM USED CARS, DEER-
LAKE, MINNESOTA, his business cards said. Within two weeks
Sylvester found an engine from a junked LeMans which used
a quart only every five hundred. He found a door, though no
trunk lid. He gave the Buick a quick coat of black enamel, inside the trunk as well, so everything matched, and had the
car on the lot stickered at $295 just in time for ricing season.

Sylvester sat in the square wooden office he had built himself. He wore a yellow shirt and a yellow tie. It was October.
Sunlight slanted through the single window. Sylvester leaned
back in his chair and smoked a Camel. His fingers smudged
the white cigarette paper. He looked out the window at the
shiny black LeSabre. He glanced at the calendar. Beth Anderson was thirty-nine this year. He wondered if she'd found a
man yet. He nibbled at a thumbnail, then stopped himself. He
looked at his hands, his fingernails. He glanced over at the
calendar again. Briefly he lifted the cellophane sheet and looked
at the tanned blonde on the beach. He looked at the untanned
parts of her. Then he let her bathing suit fall back into place,
and turned the pages to November and December. His fingers
left little black lilypads on the corners of the pages. He examined his hands again. Another three weeks, four at most,
he'd have to start work on his hands if they were to be clean
in time for Christmas. He swung around to his desk, found a
notepad and stub of a pencil. "GoJo" he wrote. After that he

doodled a minute. He drew a tall, thin girl with a long neck.

When Sylvester looked up some time later, there were Indians in the lot. A whole covey of them, like blackbirds, had lit around the Buick. Two kids perched on top of the LeSabre, another kid jumped up and down inside the lidless trunk, longer legs poked from beneath the car and several heads were visible inside the Buick.

Sylvester stood up. In the small mirror above his desk he checked his hair, adjusted his yellow tie. Then, humming a little tune he had made up himself, Sylvester stepped outside into sunlight. The Indians' hair gleamed like crows' wings.

AT THE RIVER John All Day steered the Buick backwards to the big Norway pine. When the bumper hit wood, he killed the motor and set the brake. He always parked that way to cover up the license plate and, more important, the gas cap. Sometimes on the reservation he forgot to park that way. Then his first stop had to be a gas station, which was his own fault for not parking right. Now as the bumper rocked once more against the Norway, John All Day felt the long back of the old tree come into his own body. Felt its roots in his own legs. Old Man Pine with the long legs.

The rest of the All Days, including Bobby All Day, John's brother, and several of their children, climbed out the rear windows of the black car. The kids ran to the shore and began to throw stones into the water. John and Bobby untied the canoe ropes and the long duckbill pole. They left the car radio on while they loaded the canoe.

In a still moment between songs, they heard, far out on the lake, the whump-whump of rice sticks on canoes.

Bobby straightened up to listen. "Dammit, we better hurry," Bobby said, and clattered the duckbill into the canoe.

John All Day laughed at his brother and continued to load the canoe at the same pace. Lastly he went to his wife, who was watching from the soft front seat of the black car. He put his hand on her belly. Inside, the baby kicked like a little calf. "Whoa!" John said.

His wife grinned. Her face was round and smooth and shiny, like the aspen trees on the bank, only darker and smoother, like walnut.

"Stay in the car and sleep," John said. "Honk the horn if you need me. I'll come, hey?"

"You better, mister," she said. They smiled at each other.

John and Bobby pushed off from shore. The canoe scraped on sand, then went silent on water. An Elvis song played from the black car's radio. On the shore the children waved and threw rocks after the canoe. At first their stones splashed close beside the canoe—one rock clinked on tin. "Devils!" Bobby said without looking behind him. But soon the splashes fell farther and farther behind. John All Day watched his children and the black car grow smaller. He wondered if things disappeared when they went out of sight. If they really went away.

Ahead was the rice bed, a long feather of green in blue water. As they neared the rice, John took from his pocket two pieces of pink bubble gum. He tossed one to Bobby, and they chewed the sweet gum soft. Soon the bow of the canoe entered the tall grass with a soft scraping sound. The rice stalks leaned away from both sides of the canoe. John swung his long stick and brought the rice heads over the mouth of the canoe.

"Little Mahnomen men," John said to the rice, and with his other hand brought down the flail.

Bobby poled.

John beat grain. Once a rice beard flew into the corner of his eye. Bobby stopped poling while John took the bubble gum from his mouth, held open the eyelid and pressed the gum to his eyeball. He took away the bubble gum and blinked his eye rapidly; the lake wobbled back into focus. John popped the gum back into his mouth and nodded to Bobby, who leaned into the pole. The little rice beard crunched in the bubble gum. "Mahnomen man," John said. From across the water, out of sight, came the faint laughing cries of his children and music from the black car's radio.

That afternoon at three o'clock Bobby poled the canoe slowly back toward the landing. The canoe rode low in the water.

When they came closer, John saw on the shore his two boys jumping up and down like young crows trying to fly from a tree. They flapped and called to him. "Hurry," they shouted. "The baby!"

Bobby leaned into the duckbill pole.

"In the car—" the boys shouted.

John leaped from the canoe and ran through the shallow water. From the car his wife groaned. Her feet stuck out the driver's side window. They were wide apart and her brown toes were curled like snail shells.

"It's coming," his wife said. She had bitten her bottom lip and there was blood on her chin.

"Dammit, you should have honked!" John said.

"The horn don't work," she said. She groaned again.

"It works, I tried it—" John said.

"Not for me, it don't work," she said.

"Forget the horn, man!" Bobby said from behind them.

John leaped in beside her and turned the key to start the engine. The battery clicked once and was silent.

"Goddammit!" John shouted. He tried again. Not even a click this time. Then he heard a noise, a faint faraway noise that was at the same time close up. He looked down at the dashboard. The radio volume knob was turned all the way up. He leaned his ear toward the speaker. A song. "Jesus, you listened to the radio all day!" John said.

"Why not?" she said, then groaned again.

"Why not? Why not? The damn battery, that's—"

His wife's groan rose to a shout. "It's coming, I can't stop it."

"Bobby—run to the highway—flag somebody down," John called.

Bobby's shoes kicked up dust as he ran. John knelt between her legs to help. The children gathered around.

TWENTY MINUTES later a dusty pickup jolted down the road toward the shore. Bobby rode standing up in the rear, hanging on like a bronco rider. He leaped from the truck before it came to a stop and raced forward. John came slowly from the front seat of the black car. He was grinning and holding, wrapped in his shirt, his new baby, Manny, whose full name was to be Mahnomen, which in Ojibwe meant wild rice. John's wife lay in the front seat, resting. The two biggest boys stood with pine-bough fans by the open windows of the black car and made sure no flies or mosquitos bothered their mother. The smaller kids had returned to the shore and were throwing pebbles into the water.

The pickup's driver, an older farmer with a limp, walked forward. He looked into the front seat, then at the baby. "Well, I'll be dipped," he said. He spit long and cleanly to the side, then bent down for a closer look at the baby. John held the baby forward. The farmer brought up a thick finger and touched Manny's nose. "You little bugger," the farmer said, "you little acorn, you."

John smiled and nodded.

Then the farmer looked at the Buick. "We better get your car started anyway," he said. He went to his truck and dug behind the seat for a pair of dusty jumper cables.

Bobby took up one pair of the cable grips.

"Nope—I'll do it," the farmer said. "Don't want my alternator burned out."

Bobby shrugged and let go his end.

Leaning against the big Norway pine, his bare back on the bark, John All Day held his son and watched. He felt the old man pine come into him again. Grandfather Pine. John's back was Grandfather's back, John's arms were Grandfather's thick, curving limbs, and John's baby was a pine cone, a sticky, sweet-smelling pine cone full of seeds of his own, seeds enough for a whole forest, seeds and life for anyone or anything who touched Grandfather Pine.

"Ready?" the farmer called to Bobby.

Bobby got in the driver's seat of the black car. Its rear bumper remained pressed against the big pine; from its nose, battery cables stretched forward, drooping power lines, to the farmer's truck. Bobby held up his hand.

"Here we go," the farmer called; he touched metal to metal.

John All Day felt something pass through his own body, something like the flow of river water against a canoe paddle, the way moving water pushed up through the paddle handle and into your hands and arms and shoulders and finally into your back where it turned around your spine and then you pushed it back to where it lived, where it never needed recharging or batteries or wires, that weight in the river—or in the bite of axe on wood or in a full wind against your face that pushed against you but pulled you forward at the same time—John All Day felt it pass up the chain of wood and iron and men's hands, and the black car's engine coughed alive.

After the farmer had gone, John returned the baby to his wife. Then he drove the black car down to the shore, to the canoe. He left the engine running while Bobby shoveled the rice into the open trunk. There was only one shovel, so John watched. The rice flew, each shovelful thudding onto the last, onto the rising green mound. Bobby began to sweat. "Slow down, man," John said, "you always in such a damned hurry. Running around like a damned crazy man."

Bobby straightened up fast to glare at his brother, then saw that John was smiling.

The All Days drove the black car, which sagged in the rear, out to the highway. First John took the baby and his wife home to her mother; he waited outside the house until her mother came and said everything was okay. Then he and Bobby drove fast to Deerlake to have the rice weighed while it was still wet.

The rice weighed 210 pounds.

The price was ninety cents a pound.

John and Bobby took the check and cashed it at Doc's Inn, on Main Street. The tavern was loud and warm and smelled like lake water and beer. People danced. Rice beards hung on the shirts and pants of everybody but the bartender. John bought a drink for everyone, and people clapped. Other people danced, sometimes Indians and whites together. Tiny pale-green rice worms shook loose from cuffs and pockets, and left slippery spots on the dance floor. John grinned and sipped the whiskey. He watched his brother and he watched the other dancers and he watched the beer light, a circle of seasons—spring green, summer gold, fall orange, and winter white—painted on a plastic plate turning with a grinding noise around a yellow light bulb. John watched and he chewed the bubble gum that was crunchy with rice beards and now tasted like the whiskey and now like the lake. John sipped his whiskey and he watched the dancers go around and around.

ON DECEMBER 10, Sylvester Harjula repoed the LeSabre. All Day had paid $150 down with $145 due when the rice was sold. Sylvester knew for a fact All Day had cashed his rice check at Doc's Inn—like any businessman Sylvester kept track of his customers—and Sylvester hadn't seen a dime of the $145.

Which didn't necessarily bother him. He called Ken Edevold, a high school pal who was also the deputy sheriff. He caught a lift with Ken out to the reservation. The All Day house was a white government prefab with a sagging roof and smudges all around the siding as high as children could reach. In the snowy yard sat four rusted 1966 Bonnevilles. Doors and trunk lids from three of the Bonnevilles had migrated to the blue Bonneville, which sat closest to the front door. The LeSabre sat off to the side with a drift of snow down its hood. It looked like a frozen skunk.

Sylvester knocked on the metal door. There was no storm door. Inside, a dog barked. A TV played loudly. A baby cried. Someone peeked briefly out the window, then the TV went silent. No one came to the door. Sylvester knocked again. He heard whispering. Finally he turned away and walked to the LeSabre. He had a key. He kept a key to every car he sold to the Indians and to whites as well; business was business, particularly with used cars. The LeSabre's battery was deader than an icehouse pike but Sylvester had jumper cables and a spray can of ether. Five minutes later Sylvester was driving the LeSabre off the reservation and back toward Deerlake.

In his shop Sylvester examined the LeSabre. The seats were covered with dog hair and stank accordingly. The front seat was ruined; somebody had spilled what looked like a gallon of ruby port. The trunk was covered with snow and rice hulls and frozen green worms. But none of this was a problem. Come spring he'd steam-clean the whole unit, find another front seat and a trunk lid, touch up the black enamel, and the Buick would sticker out at $325, minimum. If it didn't sell until fall, that was fine. The All Days might even buy the Buick again, which was fine by Sylvester. He felt nothing one way or the other about the All Days. They had the Buick car for ricing season, and now Sylvester had it back. And none too soon.

BETH ANDERSON rode into Deerlake on the Greyhound bus the snowy evening of December 22. Sylvester Harjula sat parked across the street in his personal car, a fully restored '51 Merc. He ran the wipers to keep the windshield clear of snow. He saw Beth get down from the bus; his heartbeat picked up RPMs. She wore a long black coat and dark stocking cap pulled low across her forehead. Her neck was bare and for a moment caught light from the street lamps. Sylvester's heartbeat picked up speed. A man came down the steps close behind Beth; Sylvester's heartbeat raced. There was some accelerator in his chest and he felt short of breath. But the headlamps of a waiting car blinked on and the man waved and turned toward the light. Sylvester, slightly dizzy, let out his breath. Beth waited for her small black suitcase, then walked, leaning into the snow, the two blocks to her mother's house.

The next morning Sylvester drove slowly by the Anderson house. He looked for tracks in the snow on the front steps, but saw none. Which was no problem. He knew her routine. He parked down the street.

At two o'clock Beth came out of the house. She swept snow from the steps, not the whole width but just enough to make a path for her own feet. She continued sweeping in this manner down the sidewalk. At the street she turned and for a long time stared at the house she had grown up in. Then she let the broom fall in the snow, and walked downtown.

Sylvester followed her in the Merc a block behind. She

looked closely at each house she passed. Once she stopped to stare up at a big elm tree, its naked branches, the white knots of snow where the black limbs joined the trunk. On Main Street Beth walked slower. She paused by every store window. Eventually she turned into Kinder's, the old soda fountain from high school days.

BETH ANDERSON took a stool at the long counter. Kinder's was empty but for two high school kids in orange-and-black letter jackets who stood jolting two pinball machines with the butts of their hands. Magazine racks to the side. Booths, probably empty, to the rear. The booths were where high school couples necked. She didn't remember ever sitting in the booth section of Kinder's.

Old Man Kinder, bald now, his mouth caved in, turned from the television set and came her way. He paused in front of her. He waited in silence. He did not recognize her.

"Cherry Coke," she said, which was the only reason she'd come here in the first place. Cherry Cokes at Kinder's did not come from a can.

Old Man Kinder turned back to the TV as he filled her glass. One rattle of ice. One long squirt of cherry that raced a red spiderweb among the cubes. Then the brown flood of cola.

She sipped the Coke. Its sweet blossom filled her nose and made it tingle. She drank half, then slowed, and looked out to Main Street. The square front windowpane was shrunken by frost to a single clear oval. A porthole in a submarine. Outside, a brown jacket passed; she saw its quilted pattern as the coat drifted by only inches from the glass, like some large, unidentifiable sea mammal.

Beth thought of Sylvester Harjula. Creepy Sylvester. He was still around, she supposed. Sylvester had been a regular at Kinder's ever since high school. Back then he had some sort of radar for her. She looked past the counter into the mirror. She took off her stocking cap and shook out her hair, except that it didn't shake. She had forgotten, again, to wash it. She replaced the stocking cap and looked away from the mirror. Mirrors were not her friends, never had been. Mirrors in truth were no one's friends, for they reflected appearance to the neglect of reality. Mirrors saw no inner life, and it was the inner life of people, other people, that had always interested Beth. She was a people-kind-of-person, always had been.

She thought of herself. Her own life. From Deerlake to a dissertation on Alain-Fournier, the doctorate, a comp/lit teaching position at Northwestern in Chicago. Not too shabby, as her students might say. Northwestern was not the University of Chicago, but with a book or two in print, anything was possible. And of course, had she been born, say, to a family of Georgetown diplomats who spoke three languages at dinner, she doubtless would be at Harvard. And often on the MacNeil/Lehrer news. One of Robert MacNeil's favorite sources, one who spoke in short but perfect paragraphs and so made his blue eyes shine; she would certainly remember to wash her hair for the "MacNeil/Lehrer Newshour."

She glanced down at the pinball players. She looked at the ceiling. An oval water stain, brown-rimmed and weepy at the corners, stared back at her. She turned to look out the frosted glass to Main Street and thought again of her own life. She had come, several years ago, to believe that Deerlake was a mistake. That, somewhat like Shirley MacLaine, she should have been born in France, preferably in 1890 in the village of Epineuil-le-Fleuriel, France. Then she would have met Alain-Fournier. They would have been childhood friends, then schoolmates; then, in adolescence, the wonderful confusion of friendship and deeper passions; and much later, because of her—Beth Anderson (though her name would have been different, perhaps Beatrice)—the drums of World World I would have sounded to Alain faint and far away. He would have remained in Epineuil. Alain, dear Alain, would have loved honor less and her more, and so would not have gone off to the front— at least not so quickly—and because of Beth and her letters, a correspondence of aesthetics atremble with desire, a correspondence surpassing even the letters between Alain-Fournier and

Jacques Rivière—all because of Beth, Alain would have returned to his writing desk. To the white paper. The dark ink.

Alain was commanding officer that day. There was ragged fire from a hostile wood. Alain had led the charge, pistol upraised; he had taken a ball in the hand or the arm, had fallen, but then risen and pressed on into the smoke, the dust, the noise. Into memory, history, dream. "Oh Alain," she whispered, "dear dark burning Alain—"

Suddenly a voice beside her said, "Beth Anderson—long time no see!"

She turned. Her mouth fell open. The dark hair across the forehead, the eyebrows, the deep-set burning eyes, the mustache. It was Sylvester Harjula.

"Welcome home," Sylvester said. He extended a chapped hand.

Beth caught her breath. Her cheeks warmed. She took the hand—there was no choice. It felt like a coconut. Like Sylvester soaked his hands in pickling brine.

"Mind if I?" Sylvester said, sitting down, leaving one stool between them.

"No—I mean, go ahead," she said. She looked back at her Coke.

They sat in silence for a while. Sylvester ordered a chocolate Coke. Creepy Sylvester.

"So when did you get in?" he asked.

"Last night."

"All by your lonesome?"

"I enjoy traveling alone," she said.

Sylvester was silent for a moment. "It's a good time to think about things, I suppose," he said.

She looked up at Sylvester. She never imagined he thought about anything except cars.

"I was thinking about you recently," Sylvester said.

Beth looked down and swirled her cubes.

"I've got the LeSabre now," Sylvester said.

In the mirror Beth saw him smile at her as if he expected to be congratulated for something. "The LeSabre?" Beth said.

"Your mother's old car," Sylvester said.

"Oh—I'd quite forgotten," Beth said.

Sylvester's smile faded. He turned back to his chocolate Coke. "Of course it's pretty well beat," Sylvester said. "Mainly an Indian car now."

Beth turned. She had forgotten about the Indians.

"Why are they so hard on cars?" she said.

Sylvester shrugged. "They don't see cars like we do. They don't care what they drive, long as it goes," Sylvester said.

Beth was silent.

"They're kind of beat down, themselves, I guess," Sylvester said. "As a race, I mean. Maybe it's like that old saying, 'you are what you drive.' "

Beth swirled her ice cubes once around her glass. "I don't have a car, so what does that make me?"

"Well," Sylvester began, "I . . ." But there was no more. His neck reddened.

For an instant Beth felt sorry for him and ashamed of herself. She shouldn't have been so quick, so sharp. All her life she'd been that way. It was not an admirable trait.

"Maybe not having a car could be good," Sylvester said. "You wouldn't have payments, upkeep, insurance."

She turned to look at Sylvester.

"You'd be more free," he said, staring straight at her.

Then her eyes fell to his lobster hands. She turned back to her watery ice cubes.

After a long silence, Sylvester said, "So how's your mother?"

"Not good," Beth said. She told him about the diabetes. The heart trouble. The forgetfulness.

THAT NIGHT, after fixing hot milk for her mother, who was, strangely, not at all sleepy by eleven o'clock, Beth finally went to bed. She was slipping toward sleep when something Sylvester had said came into her mind. Indians and cars. "You are what you drive," Sylvester had said.

Beth opened her eyes. For the Indians, a car was not a car at all, but a metaphor. A cultural metaphor. More than that: it was a Weltanschauung. And the fact that Indians cared not a whit for cars was not necessarily a sign of cultural decay; in fact, it was the opposite. Indians who drove junked cars and left them along the road when the motors burned out were the real, that is, the nonassimilated, the *true* Indians.

Beth switched on the lamp, got up and began to pace the bedroom. Of course Sylvester was right—you are what you drive. But she was right, too. She was righter. She was a writer, that is. For wrapped up in her mother's disgusting old Le-Sabre—Sylvester had told her all the details—was the whole Indian Problem.

Rapidly she dug in her suitcase for a yellow notepad and a pen. At the top of the page she wrote in bold letters "The Indian Problem, by Beth Anderson." As she waited to be visited by the next sentence, downstairs her mother gave out a groan and died.

AFTER THE funeral there was the matter of the house and her mother's belongings. For want of acquaintances her own age—Beth realized how few friends she had had in high school (not any, really)—she called Sylvester Harjula.

Sylvester appeared at her door twenty minutes later. He carried a long tool box. He said he imagined there were things of her mother's that Beth would want shipped, and he had brought along lumber, saw, hammer, nails, and strapping tape.

"Well, there is the china cabinet," Beth said.

Sylvester sawed and hammered. He made a marvelous crate; Beth found old blankets to drape the cabinet. Mid-morning, Beth made a pot of coffee. At noon they drove downtown for lunch in Sylvester's Mercury. The Mercury was scented sharply with a Pine-Tree air freshener; its seats were deeply soft and upholstered in burgundy velours, a combination Beth imagined that one might find in the waiting room of a bordello. She also realized, as they turned downtown, this was the first time she had ever ridden alone with a man her own age, in his car, down Main Street in Deerlake.

At the café she ordered a broasted half-chicken in a basket.

Sylvester ordered the same, though with potato skins rather than fries. They waited for the food in silence.

"I have a house now," Beth said to herself. She looked out the window for a long time.

Their chicken came. As they ate, Sylvester intermittently spoke, but Beth often missed what he said and didn't remember to reply. She stared out the window. Whenever she stopped eating, Sylvester paused as well. Finally she turned to Sylvester. "Would you watch the house for me? This winter?" she asked.

"Well," Sylvester began.

"For remuneration, of course," Beth said. "Then when spring comes I'll organize some sort of estate auction. However, for the short term I need someone to watch the house."

"It'd be an honor and a privilege," Sylvester said.

Beth stared at Sylvester. Then she laughed.

Sylvester's eyes widened; he looked down, into his chicken basket.

"I'm sorry," Beth said. "It's just that you sounded so . . . formal." She laughed again, and tried to cover her mouth with her hand.

"I really am very sorry," she said. She giggled.

"It's okay," Sylvester said. "I know how tough it must be."

She laughed again, louder this time, because she had entirely forgotten about her mother. She was thinking, rather, of herself. Herself, at thirty-nine years of age, sitting in Deerlake, Minnesota, picking at cold broasted chicken and fries with Sylvester Harjula of Harjula's No Problem Used Cars. She continued to laugh. She couldn't stop. She upset her water glass and laughed louder at that. Sylvester helped her up from the table and out the door into the cold air. On the way home she tipped over on the seat and kept laughing harder and harder until Sylvester realized she was crying.

THE NEXT DAY Beth prepared to leave. Sylvester had a key. Everything was in order with the electricity and water departments; the heating oil truck driver. She took a last look around the house. In the basement a faint humming noise caught her attention. She touched the furnace. The water heater. The white side of the chest-type freezer, which vibrated beneath her fingers. She had forgotten about the freezer. Ice squeaked as she lifted the lid. The freezer overflowed with large cauliflowers of frost, and beneath the frost, years' worth of food. Frozen vegetables. Meat. Berries. Packages of arm roasts, round steak, hamburger; containers of crystalline raspberries, purple chokecherries; layers and layers of hard bags of yellow corn. Among the corn was a single red coffee can which rang emptily to her touch. She lifted the can and shook it; something rustled inside with a sound like dried leaves. She pried off the plastic lid and found inside the can fifty green twenty-dollar bills. One thousand dollars in cash.

IN JANUARY, back at Northwestern, Beth happened to glance through the travel section of the Sunday *Tribune*. She began reading about sun vacations to Mexico and the Caribbean. She noticed how some of the advertisements slipped the word *singles* into their sentences; how really quite inexpensive they were.

The next day Beth booked a single's package to Club Papagallos, which meant Club Parrot, on Grand Cayman Island, which was seventy nautical miles south of Cuba. There Beth was walking along the beach with her head down to avoid stepping in the crude oil that had washed ashore and rolled itself into little black sandy balls that resembled Russian teacakes, when she bumped full-length against a tall, thin man with a Lincoln beard.

"One thousand dollars for a vacation and the damned beach is no better than a goose yard," the man said. "Look at my feet!"

Beth did.

The man was a full professor at the University of Chicago, was recently divorced, and had written two books and eighteen critical papers about Gustave Flaubert. At dinner that night he told Beth things about Flaubert that few people knew, for example, that Flaubert's saliva was perpetually blackened by mercury treatments for venereal disease. He also told Beth his former wife read nothing but James Michener, which was the straw that finally broke the back of their marriage. "Not that I didn't bring home good literature for her to read," he said twice that night.

BETH AND HENRY Ridgecraft were married in February in the office of a judge in a civic building overlooking Lake Michigan. As they left the office, Henry made a joke about the number of Chicago judges caught in recent police stings.

Beth moved into Henry's town house. And to that address, every other week, came a letter from Sylvester Harjula. Sylvester wrote on his small, brown "No Problem" stationery. His writing, always in blue ink, was cramped both in penmanship and in style, yet contained no sentence fragments or comma splices. Henry, for a good laugh, always read the letters aloud. He pointed out faint oil smudges on the pages. After a month of this Beth kept Sylvester's letters to herself.

In his letters, Sylvester wrote about the house. He said now that winter was here he worried about the furnace going out. About the pipes freezing. Since he had a key, he wrote, he sometimes slept overnight in the house. He said it was a warm house and a quiet house for sleeping, a good house all around.

Beth wrote Sylvester in return. She thanked him for being a scrupulous caretaker. She assured him that he was welcome to stay in the house, regularly if he wished. She did not, for some reason, tell him about her marriage to Henry Ridgecraft.

In his next letter Sylvester asked if she would address her letters to him in care of her mother's house. He said regular mail was important to the safety of an empty house. Also he would get her letters a day earlier, in case there was anything urgent that she wanted from him or wished to tell him. He said he hoped she wouldn't feel funny sending letters to him at her old address.

"Not strange at all," Beth wrote, though in truth it was. At first she felt as if Sylvester had become part of her family. After two or three cycles of letters, however, of Sylvester's reports and her thank-you notes in reply, Beth felt at ease writing to Sylvester at her old home address. She began to add occasional anecdotes, as she had to her mother, telling Sylvester of her students; of teaching them to write; of making them ponder, for at least fifty minutes a day, things they read.

Sylvester wrote back that he had liked Zane Grey and Jack London from school days. Now he sometimes picked up a Louis L'Amour paperback at the grocery store. He asked if she could recommend to him some books along that line.

Beth wrote back to suggest Hemingway and Faulkner, then on second thought crossed out Faulkner. She explained that Faulkner might have won the Nobel Prize but his sentences would never win any A's in her freshmen composition classes.

Sylvester wrote back and included in his letter one particularly long sentence from *The Sound and The Fury*, which he had found in the Deerlake Library. He said he could see what she meant about Faulkner. He also said that he had read *The Old Man and the Sea*. He had put the "closed" sign on his office building and read the whole book in one day. He said it was a good book, which to him meant the type of book he could see reading again sometime.

Beth wrote back immediately a rather excited letter, saying that he had hit upon the best definition of art—writing or painting or music that held up under repeated scrutiny, that got better with age. After that, Beth wrote less about the house and increasingly whatever came into mind—mostly about growing up in Deerlake. She told Sylvester things. How she had hated the choir director, Mr. Kinney, and his ugly pipe. How she thought the cheerleaders were an embarrassment to themselves. How she really had not liked school, and could not wait to turn eighteen and graduate.

Sylvester wrote that he remembered her well from school. He said it had always seemed to him that she enjoyed school. And if someone like her hadn't enjoyed school, then who ever did?

"Maybe no one," she wrote back. "Maybe no one ever is really happy with her life," she wrote. She was tired and it was late when she wrote that; when she should have been Hemingway, she was Faulkner. She wrote about her studies, about Alain-Fournier, a long rambling letter that held up her life in Deerlake to Meaulnes's life in Fournier's novel. She wrote that she, too, always felt like an outsider ". . . even to myself," she wrote. "Sometimes I feel as if there's an explanation to my life that continues to escape me; that I've missed something noble, something sublime; that in some way I have cheated myself . . . life is so strange, so harsh," she wrote.

Sylvester wrote back that he could find nothing by the Fournier fellow in the Deerlake Library, but said he was going to a used car auction at the Minneapolis Auditorium, and he would try a bigger library down there. As far as life went, he agreed it was an odd business, but he couldn't really agree with her about no one being truly happy, because here he was, Sylvester Harjula, writing letters to her, Beth Anderson. He wrote that since high school, perhaps from the first time he saw her, he had admired her more than she ever knew. He said that April first, when she was to arrive back in Deerlake, was only two weeks away, and seeing her again would make him happier than she could know.

Beth finished reading his letter and looked up from her desk. Henry knelt by his stereo grooming one of his jazz albums with an electrostatic roller; the turntable circled emptily, waiting. "Oh dear," Beth said.

BETH AND HENRY Ridgecraft drove into Deerlake in Henry's Volvo on April first. Henry had been invited to give his paper, *Window and Door Imagery in Madame Bovary*, at the University at Champagne-Urbana, but Beth had prevailed upon him to come with her to Minnesota. "Just this once," she said. For most of the trip Henry drove above the speed limit and did not look at the passing scenery.

In Deerlake, Beth directed him past the gas company, the feed mill, then across Main Street and the final two blocks to her mother's house.

Above the slouched and faintly dirty snowbanks, the wide

face of her old house looked white and fresh. For a moment
she thought the house had been newly painted; then she decided it was just the cleaner air, the brighter slant of small-
town light. The front sidewalk shone gray and wet; it was the
only bare concrete in the neighborhood.

"How does real estate move around here?" Henry asked.

"Move?" Beth said.

"Sell," Henry said, "sell."

"I . . . really have no idea," Beth said. She was looking
through the window into the living room. There were lights
on. And blue striped wallpaper. She didn't remember that wallpaper.

She walked onto the porch. The doorsill was sharp and
square, a new piece of varnished oak. The doorknob had
changed from iron to yellow brass. She tried her key. The
tumblers turned. The door swung open without squeaking. Inside music was playing. A radio. Some country-western song.

She paused to knock on the door. "Hello?" she called.
"Hello?"

The house smelled different. Gone were the brackish odors
of old carpet and furniture and stewed tomatoes. Now she
smelled fresh paint and lemon furniture wax and flowers. On
the mantel was a white vase with two red roses.

"Not bad," Henry said, steering her inside. "I'd buy this
house."

Beth's heart began to thud. She followed the hallway toward
the yellow-lit kitchen and the music. She smelled fresh coffee.
On the table were two cups and saucers and, between them, a
larger bouquet of red roses with a note.

"Where's the bathroom?" Henry called.

"Upstairs," she murmured. She stared, then turned to speak
to Henry but saw only his legs moving up the stairs, shortening as they climbed.

At the table she slowly reached down for the note. "Dearest
Beth," the small handwriting began. She crumpled shut the
note and caught her breath. There was noise behind her in the
living room. Henry—she must quickly explain all this to Henry—

so crazy, all of it, a big laugh for Henry, and of course she couldn't fault him for laughing because she was to blame really, completely to blame, she must take full responsibility for this terrible—

Then the front doorknob turned and the door swung open. Sylvester Harjula, dressed in a blue cap, a brown jacket, a pink shirt, checkered pants, all clean and pressed, stepped inside.

They stared at each other. Sylvester removed his cap. He grinned and his face reddened in the same moment.

"Sylvester—" she began, and started toward him.

"Beth—" he said. "Oh Beth." He moved toward her and his arms came up.

At that instant, upstairs, the toilet flushed.

Sylvester froze. His arms dropped to his sides. Down the stairs came Henry's brown shoes, his argyle socks, his gray wool slacks, his black belt and small potbelly, his gray sweater, his shoulders, the salt-and-pepper tip of his beard, and finally his face. Henry stopped midway to stare.

"Henry . . . Sylvester . . . Henry . . . Sylvester," Beth said. The names went around in a circle and she did not know where, on which one, to stop.

Sylvester's jaw went slack.

"Sylvester," Beth said, "this is . . . my husband, Henry Ridgecraft."

IT WAS LATE in the afternoon. Henry had made one joke about Sylvester and the roses, then went to the basement to examine the furnace. After that he went upstairs for his nap.

While Henry slept Beth sat alone in the kitchen. She made a cup of tea but drank little. She sat with her hands folded around the warmth of the cup, and watched birds come and go at the feeder.

Chickadees.

Little sparrows with red crests.

A fat blue jay that periodically chased all the small birds away.

Later she blinked as Henry stirred upstairs. The cup was cold in her hands; it was six o'clock. Soon Henry came downstairs whistling. "Hey, I'm starving," he called to Beth. "Let's go out for dinner, my treat."

He came into the kitchen with her coat. Beth stood up. She fitted her arms into the holes. Outside, they walked toward Main Street.

"Some little French place—or maybe Chinese—either will do," Henry said jovially, and put his arm around her shoulders.

It was heavy and she shrugged it off. "The Hub Café on Main Street is all that's open. It'll have to do," she said.

"Okay, okay," Henry said.

Late sunlight slanted low through the intersections and divided Main Street, already dusky in the shadow of the buildings, into a three-block lattice of blue and orange. A handful of cars, none together, sat here and there. The curved, cursive Kinder's sign hummed and clicked, then blinked on; one by one the letters flickered to pink. The final *S* buzzed, strained, but in the end could not muster itself to light.

Below the Kinder's sign, gleaming darkly, sat a long car with an orange For Sale sign taped to its rear window. Something about the car—the sweep of its fenders, the slope of the roof— did not release Beth's gaze. She squinted to see better. The black fins. The four doors.

"Hey, where you going?" Henry called.

Beth left Henry and crossed the street. A pickup with two teenagers passed. Its brake lights blinked on red as the teenagers swiveled their heads to stare at the Buick. Yes—the Buick LeSabre, their old LeSabre, the one her mother had bought, Beth realized. But it couldn't be. This LeSabre looked newer, shinier than their LeSabre had ever looked, even brand new. Slowly Beth walked closer. The Buick's paint gleamed deep obsidian black. In the curves of its chrome she saw Main Street both left and right, saw the asphalt below, saw the orange- and-purple sky above; saw her own face as if in a fun-house mirror, a wide face with round, open eyes, a face that for a moment she did not recognize. She looked behind her, but there was no one there. Only Henry across the street, and the pickup turning at the end of the block, coming back.

She turned back to the LeSabre and bent to look inside. The black seats, the dark carpet, the great jet plane dashboard with its round-eyed clock and the gleaming silver knobs—it was all exactly as she remembered. It was all the same except for, dangling from the radio dial, the Pine-Tree air freshener.

She suddenly looked up to Kinder's. In the frosted window, centered in the oval of frost-free glass, was Sylvester Harjula. He sat in profile. He did not see her because he stared straight ahead. His left hand, holding a cigarette, held up his chin. His brown eyes, unblinking, gazed far away. The only movement came from his cigarette, whose smoke curled upward white into the white frost.

"Hey, come on, I'm hungry," Henry called from across the street.

But Beth did not move. She stood in place and she stared at Sylvester Harjula. At the portrait of Sylvester Harjula. A living portrait but one already gone over into the future. As would she—she suddenly realized—if she moved from this spot. If she moved a hand, even a finger, she too would pass into her own future.

And what was that? What was her future?

She understood, with a quickness that took her breath away and which anchored her even more firmly in place, that her future was to be, quite simply, the present. Her future, if she turned her eyes or even blinked, was to remain exactly as she had always been, someone who knew the answers to everything but who had no knowledge—not one good clue—as to why or how or from where the questions ever came.

Behind Beth pickup doors slammed. Reflected in the Kinder's glass, two teenagers wearing letter jackets over sweatshirts, their gray hoods pointed up, walked quickly to the Buick. They bent to look inside.

"Man, it's cherry!" one said.

"Wonder what they want for it?" the second said.

"Plenty, I'll bet," the first said.

The closest one straightened and turned to Beth. In the shadow of his hood she could not see his face. "Hey lady," he said, "is this your car?"

ABOUT THE AUTHOR

Will Weaver is a winner of the McKnight and the Bush Foundations' Prizes for Fiction. He is also a participant in the Literature Short Fiction Syndication Program of the National Endowment for the Arts. His stories "Heart of the Fields" and "Dispersal," included in *A Gravestone Made of Wheat*, were selected as two of the Ten Best Short Stories of 1984 and 1985 by the PEN Fiction Project. He lives in Bemidji, Minnesota.